HOLOCENE

HOLOCENE

CLAYTON RUMLEY

To Natasha and my four girls;
you are my drive to be better and accomplish more.

Special thanks to Jenny Gates and all my friends and colleagues who offered their encouragement throughout the creation of this story.

In memory of my father, Bill Rumley.

Chapter 1

The relentless back and forth of the wipers did little more than push water around the windshield. Streetlights and headlights appeared fuzzy and refracted. The thumping sound of the wipers was barely audible over the din of the rainfall.

Sara sat in the back of the police cruiser as it moved slowly through the downpour towards Vatican City. She looked straight ahead, only taking her eyes off the road to glance at her phone and compare their blue position on the map with the pinned red destination.

Jean-Paul examined his wet overcoat. He gently shook off some of the raindrops and watched them fall onto his expensive Italian shoes. He looked over at Sara. Her long, dirty blonde hair, clumsily tied into a bun, continuously dripped water onto her light jacket. Her blue jeans and off-brand sneakers were also thoroughly drenched, despite having only been briefly exposed to the rain while running from the Canadian Consulate to the cruiser. It didn't seem to bother her, though. She sat rigidly upright, clutching a small photo frame to her chest with her left hand, and holding her cell phone with her right. The bags under her eyes betrayed the stress, lack of sleep, and crying that had been her companions for the previous few days.

Sara felt Jean-Paul staring at her, and when she turned to him, he quickly looked away, embarrassed.

"Can he go any faster?" she snapped impatiently.

Jean-Paul knew there would be little point in asking, but he also knew that Sara was desperate and frustrated, so he leaned forward and spoke to the driver in Italian. The young officer gestured at the weather and responded angrily; the Gendarme in the passenger seat nodded in agreement.

Sara stared blankly at the exchange, unable to understand. Jean-Paul leaned back into the uncomfortable rigid seat and sighed. "It's the weather," he explained, his slight French-Canadian accent translating the officer's rant into polite English. "Traffic is moving very slow."

As they wound through ancient and narrow cobblestone streets, Jean-Paul tried to think of something to say to pass the time, but he knew that Sara was not interested in small talk. Instead, he stared through the blanket of water pouring down his window and listened to the occasional static-filled call coming over the police radio. He wondered what he had gotten himself into.

As they neared their destination, Sara leaned forward, pushing her phone into the front between the officer and Gendarme. "*Si, si*," the officer kept replying, growing increasingly annoyed by his passengers.

When they finally arrived, the Gendarme got out first, retrieved an umbrella from the trunk, and opened it up on Jean-Paul's side of the vehicle. Jean-Paul got out, then extended a hand to help Sara from the car. The two Canadians were standing in front of a very large and old row of houses on a quiet street just inside the Vatican City walls. Looking up through the dark and the rain, Sara guessed the building was at least three stories tall. It appeared to be a residence or a small apartment complex.

Sara and Jean-Paul were led across the puddle-filled sidewalk to an awning-covered door. The officer surveilled the surroundings as the Gendarme rang the bell. A dull, warm light above the door provided a meagre source of illumination for those standing before it.

After a minute or so the door creaked open to reveal a young man dressed in dark pants and a black dress shirt with the stereotypical clerical collar. His dark, matted hair matched his solemn face. His right hand remained on the doorknob; the other was at his midsection, holding a tumbler containing a dark-coloured beverage with ice. The arm holding the glass was strangely relaxed, as if he had forgotten he was holding the drink. Jean-Paul thought he saw the glass shake a bit.

"*Si?*" the priest asked confusedly, his gaze quickly darting across the motley group at the door before settling on the Gendarme.

The Gendarme leaned toward the priest and spoke in Italian. Jean-Paul turned his head slightly to try and discern what was being said, but the sound of the rain flooded his ears with white noise.

After a brief exchange, the priest drew his free hand from behind the door and brought it up in front of the Gendarme's face, causing the Gendarme to pause mid-sentence. "Can I help you?" he called out through the weather in heavily accented English.

Sara stepped forward, slipping between Jean-Paul and the Italian police officer. She drew forth the picture frame she had been holding to her chest during the ride and turned it to face the priest. "Have you seen this man?" she asked.

The priest's perplexed gaze shifted from her face to the portrait in front of him. The photo was of a smiling young man in his early thirties, clean-shaven, with short, brown, wavy hair. Even in the low light Jean-Paul could see the colour drain from the priest's cheeks as his tumbler fell to the ground. The sound of it shattering blended into the sound of the rain.

Sara's breathing quickened and she turned with a half-smile toward Jean-Paul. In response to the glimmer of hope in her eyes, he offered a tight-lipped supportive smile, then turned back to the priest, whose gaze was still transfixed on the photograph.

"*Padre?*" Jean-Paul called out, bringing the priest's attention back to Sara.

"*Si. Si.*" the priest stuttered. He started to bring his left hand up to his mouth before realizing he had dropped his glass. He sighed in disappointment as his arm fell to his side. He again looked at Sara. "I think it's best you come in." He moved back to fully open the door. "Please, watch your step."

After the Canadians crossed the threshold, the priest stopped the police officer and the Gendarme and quietly spoke to them in Italian. Jean-Paul couldn't make it all out, but he picked up enough to know the priest was telling the officers to leave. After some polite parting words, the two men walked back out into the rain. The priest then closed the door and locked both the handle and the deadbolt, before attaching the safety chain.

With the sound of the rain relegated to a quiet whisper in the background Jean-Paul's ears adjusted to the silence and he became aware that all he could hear was the faint ticking of a clock somewhere in the darkness.

Sara instinctively bent down to slip off her sneakers, but Jean-Paul placed a hand on her shoulder. "It's okay," he quietly said. "Here in Rome visitors don't take their shoes off. The priest smiled slightly and nodded in approval. Sara tried her best to wipe her wet shoes on the modest mat just beyond the door.

"Please follow me," the priest instructed, as he walked past them and proceeded down what appeared to be a very long hallway.

As their eyes adjusted to the darkness, they could make out some intricate carvings and detailed inscriptions over and above the closed doors on their left. At the far end of the hallway, a dim light spilled from a door to the right, clearly illuminating the priest who was waiting for them. When they followed him into the room, Jean-Paul and Sara were embraced by an ancient warmth.

The ornate and spacious room served as a large den, adorned with floor-to-ceiling bookcases on every wall. The shelves were burdened by hundreds of very old, dusty, mostly leather-bound books, all accessed by a number of strategically placed ladders. Sara was drawn to the source of the warmth, a very old stone fireplace in the corner opposite the door, edged by hand-carved plinths and a wide mantle adorned with liturgical items. In front of the fireplace was a wooden coffee table flanked by an old leather couch and two worn, elegant sitting chairs. At the far end of the couch, an antique globe was open to reveal decanters, glasses, and an ice bucket. Directly before them was a large solid wooden desk covered in papers and more books.

On the couch sat another priest who looked a bit younger than the one who answered the door. He wore the same modern priestly attire and bore the same solemn look. In his left hand was a tumbler of alcohol, and in his right a smartphone. He seemed unaware that he was holding either. His demeanour didn't change as he lifted his head to look at the newcomers.

A much older priest sat at the desk. His long black hair and full beard were peppered with streaks of gray, and his eyes were bordered with prominent crow's feet. He was seated in a large leather chair that was rocked back behind the desk and wore a stern look of concentration. When he realized there were two strangers in the room, his brow furrowed further, and he quickly straightened up in his chair.

"*Cos'è questo?*" the old priest snapped.

The priest who led them into the room opened his mouth to speak, paused, then turned to Sara. "*Mi scusi signora. La fotografia.*"

It took a moment for Sara to realize what he wanted. She shook her head, trying to ground herself in this new environment. "Oh. Yes, of course. Sorry, I don't speak Italian." She then gave him the photograph.

The first priest nodded appreciatively and, without saying a word, handed it to the older priest. The man looked angrily at it, but his gaze turned immediately to shock as his eyes focused on the photograph. He dropped it on the desk and jumped up with such force that his chair rolled across the ancient tile floor and hit the bookcase behind him. Sara was momentarily distracted by the firelight glinting off his traditional, long, gold-threaded robe.

The first priest crossed his right arm to support his left elbow as his hand cradled his face in confusion. Jean-Paul looked at the priest on the couch who, though clearly puzzled by what was going on, made no effort to see what had caused such a reaction.

"*Tu chi sei?*" the old priest demanded, looking at Jean-Paul and Sara.

"English, Monsignor," the first priest corrected.

"Of course," the Monsignor said apologetically in an even thicker Italian accent, as his angry expression was exchanged for one of brief realization. "Who are you?" He then leaned in slightly to study Sara's face in more detail. "Do I know you?"

"My name is Jean-Paul Ducharme, and I'm a member of the Canadian Consulate here in Rome, though I'm acting in an unofficial capac—"

The Monsignor raised his hand to cut him off, then pointing at Sara, said, "You."

"My name is Sara Taylor."

"*Che cosa*?!" the priest on the couch said disingenuously, snapping up to the edge of the couch and causing his drink to spill out onto the floor.

Sara looked briefly at him, then back at the Monsignor. "I'm looking for my husband, Jake Taylor. He's been missing for 17 days." And then she added with a note of desperation in her voice, "Please tell me you've seen him."

"*Madonna!*" the priest on the couch gasped, making the sign of the cross.

"*Cosa facciamo?*" the first priest asked the older priest, his hands turned out in confusion. The priest on the couch also looked at the old priest for answers.

"He's asking what they should do," Jean-Paul quietly translated for Sara.

The Monsignor stared back and forth between the photo and Sara. Finally, he reached into his robes and produced a phone. He scrolled through a contact list, made a selection, then brought the phone up to his head. He held up his hand at the group, indicating that they should all wait.

"*Si, Cardinale Augusta,*" he barked into the phone. He walked out of the room, pausing at the doorway to cover the phone's speaker with his hand before turning to the first priest. "See to them," he ordered in English as he continued his exodus from the room. He resumed his conversation, his voice trailing off as he briskly walked down the hall.

The first priest turned to Jean-Paul and Sara and motioned to the couch. "Please have a seat," he said, angrily gesturing at the young priest to move. Still in shock, the priest shook his head apologetically and vacated the couch for one of the sitting chairs on the other side of the fireplace.

Sara and Jean-Paul hesitantly sat down, both grateful for the warmth of the crackling fire. Sara shivered, still cold and wet from the rain, and wishing she'd worn a heavier jacket. After a moment or two, she spoke up.

"I don't understand—"

"Forgive me!" the first priest interrupted. "My manners! My name is Father Nicolas Salvatori, but everyone calls me Father Nic." He then gestured to the second priest now sitting in the chair and drinking from his glass. "And this is Father Julien Armatti."

Father Julien awkwardly swallowed the liquor in his mouth and coughed slightly. He stood and reached out to shake Sara's hand, then Jean-Paul's. Both could feel his hand trembling.

Sara looked completely confused. "I'm sorry, but what are we doing here? Have you seen Jake or not?"

The two priests exchanged looks, with Father Julien raising his eyebrows.

"I'm afraid the only person who can answer your question is Monsignor Wowchuk," Father Nic said. Looking at Sara's blank expression, he gestured at the door. "He is the priest who just left. He'll be back."

"When?" Jean-Paul asked.

"I, I actually can't say. In the meantime, would you like something to drink? Perhaps some tea?"

Sara stuttered in mounting frustration, but Jean-Paul put his hand on her shoulder. "Tea will be fine," he replied for them both.

When Father Nic left the room, Father Julien sat back down and stared silently into his drink.

"I don't understand what's going on," Sara said quietly to Jean-Paul.

"Me neither, but it's obvious they know something, so it's probably best we wait and hear what they have to say." He leaned back into the couch, trying to relax. "To be honest," he continued in a low voice, "this is not at all what I expected."

Father Nic soon returned with a serving tray bearing a black electric kettle with steam emanating from its spout. There was a set of teacups on saucers, a sugar bowl, several varieties of tea bags, and Arrowroot cookies.

"Arrowroot?" Jean-Paul asked bemusedly, one eyebrow cocked.

Father Nic smiled sheepishly. "They're the Monsignor's favour-
ite."

At that moment Father Julien looked up from his glass and stared
intently at Sara, studying her face. "You are really Sara Taylor?" he
said in better English than the other two priests.

Sara shook her head in disbelief. "Yes, I am. Do you know me?"

"*Madonna!*" Father Julien exclaimed, ignoring her question. He
looked up at the ceiling and once again made the sign of the cross.

"*Abbastanza,*" Father Nic chided the young priest before pouring
hot water into the cups. "I think it's best we wait for the Monsignor."
He then turned his attention to the two Canadians. "Which tea would
you like?"

"Uh, any-anything is fine," Sara stuttered, trying to maintain her
composure.

"Likewise," Jean-Paul added.

Father Nic prepared two cups of green tea and served the visitors. As Jean-Paul and Sara drank their tea in silence, the two priests
went to the globe. Father Julien refreshed his drink and returned to
the chair closest to the fireplace. Father Nic took a new glass, added
some ice, and sat in the chair beside him. They joined the Canadians
in their quiet repast of tea and Arrowroot cookies. Only the sounds
of the crackling fire, the sipping of tea, and the occasional tinkling of
ice broke the silence.

Sara had almost finished her tea when the Monsignor returned,
still on the phone. He was talking rapidly, and Sara couldn't pick out
any words, not that she could understand any. Looking over at Jean-
Paul, she saw a look of shock on his face. "What?" she whispered,
leaning over to him.

Jean-Paul tilted his head toward her while still watching the Monsignor. "My liturgical Italian isn't that great," he whispered back,
"but I'm pretty sure he's talking to the Pope."

Sara looked over at the other two priests. They hadn't heard what
Jean-Paul said but based on how they were staring at the Monsignor
and the look on their faces, she concluded he was probably right.

After a few minutes and several "*Grazie*"s the Monsignor ended
the call with a final "*Amen!*". He put the phone back in his pocket with

one hand, making the sign of the cross with the other. He then leaned heavily on his desk, as if overcome by exhaustion. He soon regained his composure, and without making eye contact with anyone, walked to the globe and started preparing himself a drink.

"Can you please tell me what's going on?" Sara pleaded. "Where's Jake?"

The Monsignor finished putting ice into his glass before turning to Sara. His face softened and his eyebrows raised slightly.

"*Signora* Taylor, I will try to help you as best I can. But first, I need you to help me."

"Anything," Sara responded. Jean-Paul again detected hope in her voice.

The Monsignor finished pouring his drink, then walked over to where Father Nic was sitting. Without missing a beat, Father Nic got up to allow the Monsignor to sit, then angrily waved Father Julien out of his seat. As Father Nic claimed the now vacant seat next to the Monsignor, the young priest sneered at him before moving to the fireplace, resting on hand on the lip of the mantle.

The Monsignor pulled his phone out of his robes again, opened a voice recording app, then pressed the red record button.

"Today is May 24th, 2019," he began, before taking a sip of his drink. "I am meeting with *Signora* Sara Taylor. *Signora* Taylor, can you tell me about your husband and why you are here?"

"Okay," Sara began hesitantly. "17 days ago—"

"On May 7th, 2019?" the Monsignor clarified.

"Yeah. May 7th. My husband Jake Taylor and his best friend Darren—"

"Darren Reichert?" Father Julien blurted out excitedly.

"Yes," Sara confirmed, suddenly confused. "Wait, how do you know Darren?"

The Monsignor raised his hand at Father Julien and shot him an angry glance. "Please, no more interruptions!" he barked. "*Signora* Taylor must be allowed to tell us her story in her own words."

Sara again shook her head in disbelief before continuing. "Jake and Darren were on a two-day hiking trip in a remote ecological reserve in the province of Manitoba, where we live in central Canada.

It's called the Walter Cook Upland Caves Park Reserve, and it's a restricted area because it's sacred ground. You need a permit to go there, as well as permission from the local Cree nation. After they got both the permit and the permission, they went on their hike, and Jake vanished."

"You mean he got lost?" the Monsignor asked.

"No. Vanished. Look." Sara pulled her cell phone out of her pocket, unlocked it, then accessed the phone's messaging app. She brought up a conversation with Darren Reichert. The last message was a video attachment. She pressed play and handed it to the Monsignor. Father Nic leaned over and Father Julien moved behind them to watch. Jean-Paul got up and stood on the other side of the Monsignor.

The video revealed a clearing in the forest. The ground was broken up with irregular rock shapes and obvious caves and sinkholes. It looked otherworldly. The sounds of blowing wind, bird calls, and buzzing insects could be heard in the background.

"Wow, this is simply amazing," the recording said.

"That's Darren's voice," Sara clarified for the group.

"I know, right?"

At the sound of the second voice Father Julien quietly gasped.

"I just want to sit down and take it all in."

The video panned around to someone sitting on a limestone outcropping. He was clearly the same man as the photo on the Monsignor's desk, although his blue eyes were obscured by sunglasses. He wore faded blue jeans, hiking boots, a green windbreaker with an orange safety vest over the top, and a tan wide brim hat. His large hiking pack rose up behind his head.

"That's Jake," Sara said. The priests, wide-eyed, all nodded silently.

The video panned back over the karst landscape, then lingered for a few seconds. Suddenly the audio went dead silent. The wind, birds, and bugs could no longer be heard.

"Hey. Why is it so quiet?" Darren's voice asked, sounding much louder and clearer than before.

"Darren, do you feel that?" The video quickly panned around before settling on Jake. Suddenly a brief high-pitched whine emanated from the phone's speaker, followed by a moment of video distortion, and then Jake was gone. At the same time, water splashed onto the outcrop where he had been sitting as if someone had spilled a bucket from somewhere above. The three priests and Jean-Paul gasped quietly in unison.

"Jake?! Jake!?" The shaky video footage suggested Darren was running to the outcrop, and the last thing they heard was him frantically calling his friend's name. A few seconds later the video ended.

The Monsignor slowly handed the phone back to Sara, then leaned back in his chair, folding his hands together on his lap.

As she put the phone in her pocket, Sara explained, "Darren told me he stopped recording at that point so he could call 911. But there's no cell signal that far out, so after looking for Jake for an hour or two, he went back to the truck and drove until he got within range of a cell tower."

Father Julien retrieved his glass from the mantle and drained it while staring into the fire. As Father Nic leaned back in his chair, Sara noticed that his drink-holding hand was trembling worse than before. Jean-Paul, who had just seen the video for the first time, folded his arms and furrowed his brow as he slowly moved from behind the Monsignor.

"It has to be fake, right?" Jean-Paul asked, breaking the silence. Only Sara acknowledged his question with a sideways glance.

"Why didn't you take this to the authorities?" the Monsignor asked Sara.

"I did," Sara responded. "Well, Darren did when the RCMP showed up at the scene. They think it's fake, too, like a movie promo, or Internet publicity stunt, or something. But it's not. We've known Darren for years and he couldn't create something like this. He works in construction, not tech. He's only shared it with me and the authorities. He hasn't even posted it online or anything. What's worse is that the RCMP suspects Darren of foul play and the video as some sort of cover-up. They have search parties scouring the reserve, but they haven't found anything. It doesn't make any sense."

"Are you absolutely certain Darren didn't fake this?" Jean-Paul inquired. "Or missed seeing what actually happened to your husband? This was their first time in terrain they were unfamiliar with, right?"

"Look," Sara said, lowering her voice in frustration. "I've already said this to the police several times. Darren and his wife Trish have been our closest friends since high school. They're good people. He wouldn't do this. And there's no way he missed something. He and Trish both served in the Armed Forces and did two tours in Afghanistan before they retired early. They hunt in rural Manitoba all the time so they're familiar with the woods. Soldiers are trained to be good observers. There's just no way."

She looked at each man in the room and broke down. "This is some kind of nightmare," she sobbed, tears welling in her eyes.

Jean-Paul walked back to the couch and quietly sat beside her.

After a few moments, Father Nic asked, "*Signora* Taylor, why did you come to Rome?"

Sara wiped her eyes and retrieved her phone again while trying to compose herself. "Jake and I, we have this app we use when we go hiking or travelling. It lets us track each other's phone's GPS coordinates in real time. His last location when he went missing was north of Cedar Lake in Manitoba, before they went out of range. Like I said, no cell towers up there. But two days ago, I got a notification that he was here. In Rome. In this building. The signal lasted about a minute before it went offline again. I didn't even have time to try and message him."

The Monsignor and Father Nic both shot a stern glance at Father Julien, who pursed his lips and shrugged sheepishly. The Monsignor shook his head disapprovingly as Father Nic returned his attention to Sara. "Were the Canadian police tracking his phone also? Why aren't they here?"

Sara nodded. "They had a trace on the phone, but it only told them that the phone was in Rome. The app I have received the exact coordinates. I went to the RCMP, but they said they had to go through Interpol and that it could take over a week before they would get the clearance to investigate the signal, and possibly longer for Italian authorities to get access to the cell tower data. That's why I came as

soon as I could borrow enough money for the flight. If Jake's in trou-
ble, or hurt, or...dead, I can't wait for the police to get through the
red tape!"

"Which is where I come in," Jean-Paul added. "My cousin is a
member of the RCMP in the Manitoba detachment investigating the
disappearance. He asked me to use my connections in Rome to get
her to this location safely. I picked her up from her hotel as soon as
she arrived and brought her here."

At that moment the doorbell rang, and Father Nic hurried out to
answer it. The Monsignor stopped the recording app on his phone
and returned it to his robes.

"His Holiness has been made aware of this situation," the Monsignor said leaning toward Sara, his voice slightly lowered. "He be-
lieves, as do I, that the events that have brought you here are nothing
short of miraculous and part of a larger plan set in motion by God."

Sara and Jean-Paul exchanged puzzled glances but before they
could say anything further Father Nic returned with a man and a
woman, both in very expensive-looking jet-black suits. The man was
tall and lanky, with short black hair encircling his bald spot. He
sported a pencil-thin moustache and his long, pointed nose made
him look like a bird. The woman was at least a foot shorter than the
man, with a more robust build. Her brown hair was braided into
coils on each side of her head. Jean-Paul thought she had an almost
comically German look and was probably named "*Frau* Something-
or-Other". A briefcase was handcuffed to her wrist; the man held
several file folders against the outside of his hip.

The Monsignor continued. "It is because of this belief that the
Church is willing to reveal certain...information...to the two of you.
Are you both Roman Catholic?"

Jean-Paul half-raised his left hand. "I am."

Sara shrugged, clearly lost in the situation, but trying her best to
roll with it. "Lapsed Lutheran here," she said, with the slightest hint
of a smirk.

"I suppose it makes no difference," the Monsignor sighed, shrugging as he turned to take the folders from the man. He handed one

folder to Jean-Paul and one to Sara. They opened them simultaneously, each finding a large pile of legal documents with a gold-plated pen clipped to the topmost sheet.

"I don't understand. What is this?" Sara asked.

The Monsignor raised his left hand with three fingers showing. "There are three stories here," he replied, then lowered his hand to point at Sara. "Yours, which we have heard, was the first. The other two are here in Rome and we wish to share them with you. However, in order to do so requires me to reveal certain information that the Church normally keeps classified." He gestured at the folders on each person's lap. "Those are non-disclosure agreements. In layman's terms they state that you are not to reveal anything you see, hear, or read from this point forward to anyone. Ever."

"And if we do?" Sara asked, bewildered.

"For non-Catholics the penalty is that the Church will deny everything and sue you into Oblivion for defamation. "And for Catholics," the Monsignor continued, narrowing his eyes at Jean-Paul, "excommunication." He paused briefly and smiled. "And then we'll deny everything and sue you into Oblivion for defamation."

Sara turned to Jean-Paul, her face twisted in perplexity. "None of this makes any sense. I don't even know why I'd sign this. Do I need a lawyer?" Then she demanded of the Monsignor, "Do you know where my husband is or not?"

The Monsignor softened his features and sighed. "*Signora* Taylor, I may not be able to give you any answers that will satisfy you. In fact, you will likely end up with more questions when we are done. All I can promise you at this point is information."

Sara could see that Jean-Paul looked as perplexed as she did. All he could do was shrug. She exhaled loudly, slouching forward over the stack of papers. "I guess I don't have a choice," she sighed, as she started initialling pages. "I need answers, and if this is the only way…" The bird-faced man in the suit watched them both intently as they wrote, promptly pointing out any missed spots.

When final signatures were done, and the documents notarized by the woman with the case, the folders were returned to the man, who then produced a set of keys and unlocked the handcuffs. The briefcase was placed on the desk and the mysterious man and woman left. The Monsignor opened the case and pulled out two plastic security cards hanging from lanyards. Sara and Jean-Paul read the word "*provvisorio*" that was printed in all-capital red letters across the cards. SAs they each put one of the lanyards around their necks, Sara twisted hers so she could see the front more closely. "It says 'temporary'," Jean-Paul whispered.

The Monsignor walked back to his desk and reached somewhere underneath. A soft "click" was heard in the room, and after picking up the briefcase, he turned and walked over to one of the bookcases. When he pulled on it, it swung open, revealing a hidden access with ancient stone walls. Fluorescent lights started flickering, lighting up a narrow staircase leading downward. The modern lights illuminated dark patches on the walls once occupied by candles or torches, and the humming of the ballasts echoed and were amplified in the small space. The Monsignor beckoned the Canadians to follow him as he started down the stairs. Fathers Nic and Julien followed behind, with Julien closing the case behind him.

As he descended, the Monsignor wistfully ran his free hand along the stones in the wall. "These were laid near the end of the reign of Constantine the Sixth. They have survived for thirteen hundred years, yet such is but a moment in the grand scheme of things."

At the bottom of the stairs was another hallway that stretched five or six metres. At the end, a large metal door stood waiting with a security pad beside it. The Monsignor paused at the door to fish out his security card from his robes. He pressed it against the sensor, and after a beep and a click, he pulled open the door to reveal a small corridor with two armed guards on either side. Beyond them was yet another door, similar to the first. Passing the guards without acknowledging either of them, the Monsignor continued straight ahead. The guards made it clear they were looking closely at the temporary badges around the Canadians' necks.

Using his card on the security pad, the Monsignor unlocked and opened the second door. Sara and Jean-Paul were immediately greeted with a strong gust of cool, dry air. The stark room they entered was quite the contrast to the ancient stone tunnel they had just passed through. It was bright and white, with stainless steel tables, computers, and a large projector screen. As the door closed tightly behind them, Jean-Paul could feel a change in the air pressure. Gone was any sensation of the humid outdoors and the musty dampness of the stairwell and corridor.

"What is going on?" Sara asked quietly, to no one in particular.

The Monsignor motioned at Father Nic, who nodded and walked into an adjoining room. A few moments later he returned with a small glass case that he put on the table in front of the group. Father Julien nervously fidgeted at the sight of it. Inside, resting on the plastic base was a disassembled smartphone in several pieces. The screen had a large crack in the front. Sara's eyes immediately went wide.

"Oh God," she choked as she tugged on Jean-Paul's arm. "It's Jake's phone! That's the custom phone case I got him for his birthday last year!" She looked at the Monsignor and angrily started toward him. "Where did you get that? Where is Jake? Is he here?"

The Monsignor pursed his lips, but stood his ground. "*Signora*," he spoke, struggling to find the right words, "I do not know where he is."

Sara dropped her trembling hands to her side, clenching them into fists to steady them. Jean-Paul noticed the action, and wondered if she was preparing to use them. Lowering her voice, Sara quietly but sternly asked, "Is…my…husband…dead?"

"I…I can't answer that," the Monsignor responded just as quietly.

"I can't deal with this! I just want some answers!" Sara cried out in frustration as she slumped to the floor, her voice echoing in the large room. Jean-Paul quickly reached down and helped her up while Father Nic fetched her a chair.

The Monsignor brought over another chair and placed it in front of Sara. He sat down, while Father Nic instructed Father Julien to fetch tissues for her. Father Julien dashed down the hall at the end of the room and returned with a box, which he gently held out to the grieving woman.

"Thank you," she croaked through tears as she took a tissue and cried into it.

Jean-Paul turned his attention back to the Monsignor, taking a step toward him. "How did you get Jake Taylor's phone?" he angrily demanded. "How did it get here?"

"That is not an easy question to answer," the Monsignor started, then quickly continued. "But what I can tell you is that when we were investigating the phone, Father Julien, who is from the Vatican's IT department, got a little overzealous and decided to simply plug the phone into a charger. Much to our surprise, the phone powered up for a minute or two before...what exactly happened, Father Julien?"

Father Julien perked up. "A capacitor on the phone's mainboard blew and it lost power. Though, as we know now, it was up long enough to connect to the nearest cellular tower and transmit its GPS coordinates to you, *Signora* Taylor."

Feeling an angry glance from the Monsignor, Father Julien briefly grimaced and looked down at the floor in shame.

The Monsignor then confirmed, "We were afraid the phone was completely destroyed, but fortunately we were able to retrieve the data from it."

Father Julien perked up again and interjected. "It was really clever. We created a direct interface to the internal memory by by-passing—"

"I don't think they care about the technical details," Father Nic snapped.

Sara sniffled and sat up. "Wait, you said 'data'. What data? You got data off Jake's phone?"

"*Si*," the Monsignor said while nodding. "We got it all this morning and had just finished reviewing it before you showed up."

"Now hold on," Jean-Paul interrupted. "You still haven't explained how you got his phone. How did it get to Rome? Where is Jake Taylor? And if he's dead, where's his body?"

"I told you there were three stories here," the Monsignor calmly replied. "We've heard *Signora* Taylor's story and now it is time to hear the second story...from Jacob Taylor. He will provide a better explanation than I can."

The Canadians exchanged puzzled looks while the Monsignor nodded at Father Julien. The younger priest then walked across the room to a laptop on a podium at the back. He pressed some buttons and a data projector hanging from the ceiling turned on as the lights in the room dimmed. Once the projector had started up and connected to the laptop, the group was looking at a screen with a folder entitled "Jacob Taylor". It was filled with files ending in '.jpg' or '.avi'.

"These images and video files were retrieved from your husband's phone," Father Julien began. He opened the first whose name started with "20190504" for May 4, 2019. It was a photo of Sara and Jake together on a couch.

"Yes!" Sara exclaimed. "That was taken in our living room a few days before he went on his trip."

"We figured that was the case," Father Julien said to himself out loud, as if he had just solved some great mystery.

The next few photos were of Sara and another woman, a pretty Filipina, sitting on the same couch, her long, black hair pulled back into a ponytail. They were both smiling at the camera. "That's Trish, Darren's wife," Sara explained. "They both came over the morning Darren and Jake left. I remember Jake snapping that photo while we were hanging out in the living room. If I remember correctly, Jake made us take a group photo right after that."

The Monsignor nodded in agreement as the next image came up. It showed Jake, sitting on the couch next to Sara, dressed in the same jeans and T-shirt he was wearing when he vanished. Beside her was Trish, and finally another man who, by process of elimination, was Darren. He was tan and muscular, with short-cropped hair. Part of an indiscernible tattoo peeked out below the sleeve of his T-shirt on his left arm. Everyone in the picture was smiling and happy.

Father Julien resumed narrating as he clicked through the pictures like a slideshow. "As you can see, the pictures continue with him going on the trip with Mr. Reichert to the reserve." The images started outside Jake and Sara's house in Winnipeg, and alternated between pictures of scenery, selfies, and photos of Darren, who was driving. Urban and suburban scenes gave way to farmland and forest as they travelled further north up Highway 6 to the bush trail leading to the Walter Cook Upland Caves Park Reserve. Father Julien paused longer on images taken as Darren and Jake hiked through the reserve. Those were of the karst landscape, limestone cave entrances, and Darren smiling, backdropped by the strange setting.

Father Julien finally stopped on a photograph of Darren standing off in the distance, holding his phone at arm's length, clearly recording a video with the rocky ground beyond him in the background.

Sara squinted at the image, sensing something familiar about it, then pointed at the screen.

"That, that's the spot where Darren took his video, right? That's the same clearing!" She took out her own phone and brought up the video Darren had sent her, pausing it at the point he had been panning the scenery with his back to Jake. She held the phone up in front of the projector screen and the others gathered around to compare the two.

"I thought it looked familiar," Father Nic muttered while shaking his head in disbelief.

"So, Jake took that photo from the spot where he disappeared?" Jean-Paul asked.

Father Julien returned to the podium. "It looks like it, yes," he replied before pausing for a moment and drawing a long breath. Nodding his face toward the photo on the screen, he continued. "That was the last photo Jacob Taylor took at the reserve, but it's not the last file on his phone."

With all eyes glued to the screen, Father Julien pressed the right arrow key on the laptop to advance to the next file. The projector screen's image changed to the first frame of a video. It showed Jake standing with forest behind him, his orange vest filthy and torn. The clean-shaven face from the previous photographs wore a few days of beard stubble, and there was a large cut across his forehead over his right eye. A trail of dried blood led away from the cut, ending partway down the side of his face.

"Oh my God!" Sara exclaimed in shock, bringing her hands up to her mouth.

The Monsignor reached over and placed his hand on Sara's shoulder. "This," he said sternly, but with a slight tremble in his voice, "this is where things get strange. Are you prepared for what comes next, *Signora* Taylor?"

To still her trembling bottom lip, Sara tightly closed her mouth, then looked directly at the Monsignor. He read her answer in her eyes, then nodded to Father Julien. Everyone looked at the screen. Father Julien took a deep breath and pressed play.

Chapter 2

The paused frame sprang to life. The sound of wind buffeting the phone's microphone filled the lab's speakers. Jake could be seen breathing heavily and the small leaves on the trees behind him fluttered in the wind.

"My name is Jake Taylor. Three days ago I was hiking north of Cedar Lake when something happened. I think I fell into a sinkhole and got swept along an underground river for some distance because one moment I was sitting there and the next I was under water. I managed to get to the surface and to the shore here."

He turned the camera away from him and panned it along the shoreline before him. A beach of small polished rocks led from the waterline before transitioning to grass, brush, and trees. Despite it being broad daylight there was a thick fog that made the scenery disappear into a grayish-white haze a few dozen metres away in any direction. "I think I'm on Cedar Lake but this fog has been heavy like this since I got here and I can't see anything."

He turned the camera back to his face. "Luckily my phone is water resistant and I didn't lose it underwater. I waited until it was dry, though, before turning it on. There's no cell coverage up here so of course I don't have a signal but the water must have messed with my phone because my clock is out of sync. It says it's 3am now when it's clearly sometime around noon."

Jake directed the camera at a small fire pit and a simple lean-to shelter made of branches and fern leaves a few metres from the shore. "I've done what every good lost hiker should do and stayed by water and in one spot. I've also kept the fire going as much as possible, but I'm guessing the fog is making it difficult for any Search and Rescue teams looking for me."

The image spun around until Jake's face was back on the screen. "Oh! I was hiking with my best friend Darren Reichert when we got separated. I hope he's okay."

He reached his index finger out to the screen, apparently touching his phone. "My battery is almost dead so I'm going to stop the recording soon. Luckily I have this," he pointed the camera at his backpack and reached inside, pulling out a large rectangular array of solar cells. "This is a solar phone charger. Always good for a hiker to have in case they get lost. Once this fog clears up I'll recharge my phone, try to get my bearings, and hopefully get the attention of a rescue plane or a boat."

Jake moved back to his campsite and sat down. The small fire's crackling could be heard in the background. "I decided to start making video recordings because it's been three days and I'm getting worried," he said, his expression turning grim. "Right now I have plenty of water and emergency ration food Darren brought with us for the hike...thank goodness for his military training. There are also blueberries in the bush here which should keep me alive for a while after that. But if anything should happen to me and you find this phone, please let my wife Sara know I'm sorry and I love her. Love you, babe."

Jake drew his left hand up to his mouth, kissed his index and middle fingers, then reached out and touched the screen, stopping the recording. The video playback froze on this final frame.

All eyes in the room were transfixed on the image. Only the Monsignor looked away, in order to hand a tissue to Sara, who was choking back tears. His movements startled her and she snapped back to reality. "Wh-why haven't you given this to the police? We could be using this to find him...or if he's dead...at least recover his body."

The Monsignor sighed and rubbed his eyes with this thumb and forefinger, allowing them to meet and rest briefly at the bridge of his nose. "I'm afraid it wouldn't help. That much will become apparent if we watch the rest of the videos. Would you like to continue?"

Sara nodded, clutching the tissue to her upper lip. The Monsignor looked back at Father Julien who advanced to the next video and played it.

Jake once again appeared on the screen. The stubble on his face was thicker and his eyes looked fatigued. In the background the fog was gone, and the rocky beach gave way to water that stretched to the horizon. Only a thin, dark line in the distance indicated there was land across the water. "Hi, it's Jake Taylor again," he began. "So it's day six since I got here. Yesterday afternoon the fog finally cleared up and I was able to charge my phone to 75%. I've turned off wifi, bluetooth, and most background apps to make my phone last as long as possible."

The camera spun away from him to show everyone what he was seeing. The shore he was standing on dropped off quickly into the vast lake. "So I came up about twenty or thirty metres over there," he said while pointing out into the water. "Now that I can take a good look around I'm pretty certain that I'm on a small island on Cedar Lake. Or some other lake nearby. This is the north shore. Now hold on a second..."

The recording ended and Father Julien advanced to the next video, this one with Jake's face filling the screen again. Without waiting for permission, he pressed play.

"...and *this* is the south shore," Jake resumed, panning the camera away once more. Like the north shore, the south shore's beach was made up of small, water-polished rocks that disappeared into the dark blue depths of the lake. Unlike the north shore however, was the land across the water. It was much closer than anything visible in the north and the viewers in the room could make out individual trees between the water and the blue sky.

"That's mainland right there," Jake announced while he slowly panned the horizon. "It's one, maybe two kilometres away. I'm fairly certain I can make that swim."

The scene jolted and began bobbing up and down as Jake started walking back northward. Ahead was his campsite. He continued talking as he stepped awkwardly on the rocky shore. "I know that you're supposed to stay in one spot, but it's been six days and I haven't seen any sign of a rescue party. Hell, I haven't seen any or heard any boats or aircraft at all, for that matter. So I've decided my best bet is to head south. Sooner or later I'll hit Highway 60, which runs between Cedar Lake and Lake Winnipegosis. Even if I somehow miss the highway, there's got to be cell service in Easterville or Grand

Rapids and eventually I'll get close enough to civilization that I'll be able to call for help."

As he reached the campsite he panned over his possessions which were laid out on the ground next to the campfire. "Here's what I've got; my water-resistant backpack, my hat, my sweater, a first-aid kit, a small mirror, a compass, a magnifying glass, my solar charging panel, a few granola bars that I've been rationing, a couple of emergency rations, a couple of waterproof lighters, and some spare socks and underwear. I've also held onto the plastic sandwich bags I brought my lunch in. I'll store some berries in them and take them with me."

He reached into the backpack and pulled out some plastic bags. "There's also a couple of plastic shopping bags here. I'll strip and store my clothes and boots in the bags. Hopefully they'll stay relatively dry because it took a few days by the fire to dry my boots when I first got here."

His face reappeared on the screen. "Now, I'm still working under the assumption that Search and Rescue is out there looking for me. So if they find this campsite I'm going to leave them some bread-crumbs to follow." He pointed the camera at the ground where several of the lighter-coloured rocks had been collected from the shore and arranged to make a large arrow pointing south. "I'm going to do this on the south shore too before I leave, so they know what direction I was headed in."

He turned the camera back to his face. "I'll try to get some rest tonight, and then tomorrow morning I'm leaving," he said. The recording stopped, freezing once again on his face.

The Monsignor gestured for Father Julien to wait a moment before starting the next video, while placing his other hand on his stomach. Looking at the floor he said "*Scusa!* I get a little bit of motion sickness whenever he's walking and filming."

Sara shifted impatiently while the Monsignor's stomach settled. Father Nic leaned over to Jean-Paul. "He was the same way when we watched *The Blair Witch Project* at the Vatican theatre," he whispered.

After a minute or so the Monsignor regained his composure and nodded at Father Julien to continue. The next video sprang to life, once again with Jake's face filling the screen. He looked more rested and determined. He pushed a hand through his hair as he started talking. "It's now day seven and I'm ready to get off this island. Dawn was about an hour ago. It's late spring but it's been pretty chilly and the water is even colder, so the sooner I get across the shore, the sooner I can build a fire and get warm.

"Oh hey, check this out," he exclaimed as he pointed the camera back to the land at the horizon and the image became blurred as the camera adjusted its focus. Above the trees was a dark cloud that appeared to be moving. As the scene came into focus it revealed the cloud to be a huge flock of birds settling in the trees. "I know it's spring and all the birds are coming back, but given how far away I am, that's got to be a huge flock of some kind of bird. I didn't see anything like that on the drive up here."

The camera was directed to the ground where another stone arrow pointed south. Also visible from this angle was the fact that he was completely nude.

"Oh...ok," Jean-Paul said in awkward surprise. Sara snickered slightly, allowing herself a moment of levity.

"As you can see, I've gone *au naturel* for my little swim. Originally I was going to swim in my underwear but I'm going to want dry clothes when I get across to the other side and it's not like anyone's around to see. So if I don't make it and you find my naked-ass body, that's why," Jake said, chuckling. "I hope some big sturgeon doesn't mistake my junk for a worm!"

The scene panned to the water's edge where a large piece of driftwood rolled back and forth against the rocky beach, pushed by the small waves. "I'm going to use that piece of wood as a floatation device. I figure it'll help me keep my head and backpack above water so I can just use my legs to kick and swim. I'm not the best swimmer but I think I can make it across to the other side."

He turned the camera back to face him. "Love you, Sara. See you soon," he said. The screen froze as the recording stopped. The slideshow remained on that file for several seconds.

"Did he make it?" Sara asked while turning to Father Julien, breaking the silence of the room.

Father Julien seemed to be lost in thought but snapped back to reality at the sound of Sara's voice. "Oh! *Scusa!*" he exclaimed as he advanced to the next video and hit the play button.

The next video started with Jake holding the cellphone in the air above him as he lay on a large rocky surface, still naked. His hair was wet and there were droplets of water on his body. He shivered and panted as he spoke. "Well, I made it. Either the shore was way further than I estimated or the current was really strong...or some combination of the two...but I'm across. It took a few hours, but I'm across. I'm pretty much done, so I'm just going to let the sun dry me off for a bit before I get dressed." A large shiver passed through his body. "Damn that water was cold!" he exclaimed. "At least the sandwich bag did its job and kept my cell phone dry this time."

Jake reached up and pushed his wet hair back and ran his hand around his jaw, wiping away the water from his whiskers. "Once I've caught my breath and dried up a bit my next step is to set up a new camp here on the shore. I'll get a fire going and get some rest. That swim took a lot out of me and I'm not going anywhere right now." He reached into his backpack and pulled out a granola bar. "I know I'm supposed to be rationing," he said as he took a bite, "but I really need some carbs." The recording ended just as he started taking a second bite.

The next video started, and it was noticeably darker than the previous one, with the sky behind Jake coloured red at the horizon. He was dressed and wearing his hat. "So that swim took a lot out of me and I've slept most of the day away, but I stayed close to the fire and I'm feeling much better. I think hypothermia was avoided. There were more berries close to the shore here so I've had some more to eat. There was also a lot of sun today so my phone is almost completely charged again."

Jake paused in his talking and broke eye contact with the screen to look around him. "It is crazy peaceful here. Nothing but bird calls and a few of spring's first insects. You know, I had recently taken up meditation to try and destress but despite everything going on it's so peaceful here I haven't felt the need to at all. I've also seen a lot of fish jumping in the lake. Too bad I don't have a fishing rod...not that I was much of a fisherman anyway. Not like Darren. This would be a nice place to visit if I wasn't lost."

He lowered his head, removed his hat, rubbed his brow and returned the hat to his head. "So I've been thinking about how it's been seven days now. Darren would have altered the authorities. Hell, even if Darren was lost too, Sara and Trish would have raised Hell. But I still haven't seen any sign of rescue. I'm thinking this might not be Cedar Lake; maybe I was swept north instead of south. That would explain why I haven't seen or heard any planes or boats...I'm somewhere even more remote than I thought."

He paused, and tightened his lips in determination. "Regardless, heading south is the right thing to do. Civilization is south....God...I hope they've found Darren and that he's okay." He looked directly into the camera for a moment before his hand reached up and stopped the recording.

The next video file started up with Jake's face surrounded by branches and leaves. "Good morning, today is day eight," he said. He panned the camera to show he was about three metres up a large elm tree. "I suppose you're wondering why I'm up in a tree?" he asked, turning the camera back to his face. "I've decided I need more protein in my diet than what the berries are giving me, and I don't know enough about wild mushrooms to know which are safe to eat, so I've decided to have eggs for breakfast."

He panned the camera to the branch in front of him. There in the crotch of the branch was a small nest made out of twigs and branches arranged similar to a large spider web. In the centre was one small egg. "This nest belongs to one of the birds from that giant flock I filmed yesterday," Jake explained as he reached into the nest to retrieve the egg. "The male...I guess he was the male because he was brightly coloured...flew away but I got a good look at him. Looks a bit like a mourning dove or a pigeon. I've seen flocks of pigeons before...but the sheer number of them is insane. There must be thousands. I've never seen anything like this. And they fly really fast! I'm going to stop here so I don't drop the phone while I'm climbing down."

The next video started up with Jake propping the phone up against something unseen and moving back to sit down on a fallen tree a couple of metres away. It was the first time he was fully in frame and Sara gasped at his appearance. His clothes were stained and covered in debris. His hat was similarly soiled and the brim was no longer even. His forearms were heavily scratched up and his boots were caked in mud. "Well," he said, grimacing. "I've never had raw egg before, but I don't have anything to cook it in. I just have to keep telling myself I need the protein if I'm going to keep alive."

He tilted his head back and cracked the egg open and let the yolk fall into his mouth, swallowing quickly. "Oh god, that was gross," he sputtered as he discarded the shell and wiped his mouth with the back of his hand, "but I did it."

He knelt onto the ground and crawled over to the phone, picking it back up. "I'm going to grab a few more eggs from the other nests around here, and if I can I'll snap some pics of these birds. Then I'm going to go pack up my camp and continue south." He reached towards the screen and the video stopped.

The next fourteen slides were still photos of the birds. Groups of them in trees, individuals in nests, and a few he got fairly close up to. The females were smaller and a mix of brown and gray with a few spots on their wings. The males were bigger and had a reddish breast, similar to a robin.

"They're very pretty," Sara said.

"Indeed. In fact, those are—" Father Nic began before the sharp gaze of the Monsignor caused him to stop.

"All in good time, *Padre*," the Monsignor admonished his junior. Father Nic closed his eyes and nodded before waving at Father Julien to proceed.

The next video started with Jake swatting away at some flies that were buzzing around him as he walked through the brush. With each step the forest in the background shook in a blurry haze, but as long as everyone kept their eyes on Jake it wasn't too distracting. Jake's eyes darted between the camera and the ground in front of him as he tried to watch where he was going.

"So a lot of things have really started to bother me. I know I'm in a remote area as far as Manitoba goes, but there are still communities here. There are people who hunt, fish, trap...drive snowmobiles and quads...but I haven't seen any evidence of trails that aren't animal trails. And garbage! Even when we were at the cave reserve we saw beer cans and plastic bags on the ground. I haven't even seen a single Timmie's cup."

The Monsignor gestured to Father Julien to pause the recording, who immediately complied. He looked at the two Canadians. "Timmie's cup?"

"Tim Hortons," Sara replied.

The Monsignor's confused expression didn't change.

"They're a national coffee and donut shop chain in Canada," Jean-Paul clarified. "A lot of people throw the cups on the ground. They're very distinctive."

The Monsignor appeared satisfied with the explanation and nodded at Julien to continue. Father Nic took out a small notepad and pen and wrote something down.

Jake waved off a few more flies that were buzzing between him and the camera. "I've been walking due south for about three hours now. I've been trying to move quickly, but even if I'm only going around five kilometres per hour I should have covered between ten and twenty kilometres. I studied the satellite maps around the cave reserve before we left. I know there are roads that run just south of Cedar Lake. Why haven't I crossed any? If I got swept away by some underground river, how far could it have taken me? Why didn't I drown? Why did it seem like no time passed between when I fell and when I realized I was underwater? Did I black out?"

He waved away the flies once more as he glanced down to watch his footing. "I keep leaving arrows made of wood or rock in case search parties are looking north of here. Why haven't I seen any search planes or helicopters yet? Or heard any for that matter?"

Jake stopped walking for a moment and leaned on a birch tree while he caught his breath. "Oh yeah, I forgot to mention this before.

The first night after the fog cleared I woke up to stoke the fire and decided to stargaze for a while. Now I've watched a few meteor showers with Darren but I've never seen anything like what I saw that night! There must've been several hundred in the hour or so I watched! And big ones! This isn't the time of year for a meteor shower, either. The Leonids and the Perseids are the biggest showers of the year and they don't happen in the spring."

He resumed his walking and the background resumed shaking behind him from the motion. "And there's one more thing; satellites. I didn't see any. Normally on any given night if I stare at the sky long enough I'll see one or two...sometimes several. I haven't seen one since I got here. Now this is going to sound insane, but what if some sort of disaster has happened? What if those weren't meteorites but our satellites burning up in the atmosphere? What if the reason I can't get a cell signal or a GPS lock is because there's been a war...or God forbid...an alien invasion or something and all our tech has been destroyed?"

Jake stopped walking and shook his head dismissively. "No, that doesn't make any sense, either. Where are the roads? Even if they were destroyed there'd be craters or something."

Suddenly the scene darkened and a loud commotion caused him to look up. He turned the camera skywards. Through the tree branches and leaves were the movements of hundreds of black shapes, blotting out the sky. "And where did all these damn doves come from?!" he called out over the noise.

Turning the camera back to his face his eyes grew wide with grim realization. "Maybe...I'm dead," he said solemnly. At that moment something bit the back of his neck, causing him to cry "ouch!" and slap himself. He brought his hand up to the camera to display the crushed insect on his palm. "No, I'm pretty sure I'm not dead," he sighed in relief, regaining his composure. "On the plus side, I think the terrain is sloping downward a bit". The playback stopped.

While the video was frozen on that last frame, Jean-Paul took a moment to look around the room. The others were staring at the screen awaiting the next video to start, but the priests looked apprehensive and at that moment he realized that they knew something was about to happen. Father Julien advanced to the next video but before Jean-Paul turned back to the screen he saw Sara's eyes widen and her face blanche.

On the screen was Jake, his eyes wide and his face frozen in a moment of terror. Jean-Paul could hear Father Julien take a deep breath before he started the video.

Jake was leaning against a tree and panting heavily. He kept looking over his shoulder at something unseen as he spoke in a frantic whisper. "Oh shit! Oh shit! Oh shit! I think I'm going insane. I think I've had a mental breakdown...or this is just a bad dream...or...or I'm hallucinating. Yeah...there was something in the water...or the air...or those eggs I ate yesterday."

The sound of a branch snapping in the distance caused him to cower behind the tree for a moment before he continued.

"Okay, okay. This is what happened. I heard some noises up ahead, like something big moving through the brush and breaking branches. I saw lots of deer today but this sounded bigger and I thought it might have been a bear."

He stopped talking to rub his forehead and then slap his cheeks as if he was trying to wake himself up. He shook his head and focussed back on the camera. "Now what are you supposed to do if you think there are bears when you're out hiking? Make lots of noise. I yelled, clapped my hands, whistled, but it didn't run away or anything. So I very carefully walked up to check it out and...oh shit...look. I know I've lost it, okay. This is what I'm going to do: I'm going to film this with the camera, then I'm going to watch the video, see that there's nothing there, and know that I'm hallucinating. Okay?"

He nodded in response to himself and took a deep breath. "Okay. Here we go."

He pointed the camera ahead of him as he proceeded. In addition to the sounds of his movements were the sounds of large branches being broken in the distance. As the noises got louder Jake slowed his approach until a figure could be seen ahead through the brush. He moved sideways to approach the figure from a wide angle, keeping the camera pointing at it. Eventually he reached the edge of a small clearing. The image was shaking and he muttered quietly about his hands trembling. As he panned the camera a large, brown, blurry creature came into view. It initially appeared to be a bear, and was certainly the size of one, but as the camera focussed it revealed a small hair-covered elephant with ears that looked too tiny for its head and little tusks poking out on either side of its mouth. It was reaching up with its trunk to pull leaves off one of the trees at the edge of the clearing in which it was standing, snapping the branches as it did so. It curled its trunk up and placed the leaves in its mouth.

"I am seeing this in real life and on my phone right now! That is not a hallucination! That is a woolly mammoth!"

The small creature grunted as it chewed on the leaves loudly. Jake kept the camera on the creature for several seconds until a loud blast like a trumpet offscreen caused the scene to shake as he jumped from the noise. The image panned to the right, revealing an enormous mammoth at the far side of the clearing with giant tusks. Responding to the call, the calf left the tree and crossed the clearing quickly to get back to the larger one. They proceeded to walk out of the clearing, both of them grunting at each other.

"That must have been the mom," Jake whispered excitedly off-screen as he followed the edge of the clearing, keeping himself just within the brush. Suddenly the phone poked through the last of the brush and froze, as Jake and everyone else watching in the room gasped in unison. Before them was a massive expanse of prairie grass filled with a herd of similar mammoths; males, females, and calves, grazing and trumpeting. The camera was suddenly pointed to the ground as Jake could be heard exclaiming "my God!". After a minute or so of the ground being recorded Jake said "Oh! shit!" and brought the phone back up to face him. "I...I need a minute or two," he said, stopping the recording.

"Mammoths?" Jean-Paul asked incredulously. Sara sat staring at the screen in bewilderment.

"Mastodons, actually," Father Nic replied. He got up and walked up in front of them, showing them a tablet he held in his hands. On it was a picture of two hairy elephants, the one on the right resembling the creatures in the video and the one on the left being much larger. Father Nic pointed to the one on the left. "This is a woolly mammoth," he said, and moved his finger to the smaller creature on the right, "—and this is a mastodon."

"That...that's impossible," Sara said. "Those creatures are extinct."

"Yes," Father Nic said, as he tapped on the tablet to switch screens. "And so are these."

The tablet now displayed the Wikipedia entry for the passenger pigeon. Jean-Paul leaned in and looked over Sara's shoulder as she took the tablet and started scrolling through the entry. Artist recreations, photographs of stuffed specimens, and a few black and white photos of the last remaining birds...all of them looked like the birds from the photos and videos Jake had taken.

"The last passenger pigeon is believed to have died around 1914," Father Nic spoke in a lowered voice. "Prior to European colonization it is believed that there were three to five billion of them in North America. Their flocks were reported to have been so huge as to black out the skies."

Sara attempted to come to terms with the information before her. "So wait...are you saying Jake has gone back in time?"

Jean-Paul snorted dismissively. "That's ludicrous!"

"As crazy as it sounds, I'm afraid that such is our conclusion," the Monsignor said seriously.

Sara sat dumbfounded.

Jean-Paul grew frustrated. "This has got to be a hoax," he gestured at the screen. "It's...it's computer-generated or something!"

The Monsignor shook his head. "No. It is real."

"How can you be sure?" Sara asked.

"Because," the Monsignor said, leaning back into his chair. "The Catholic Church has had your husband's mobile phone in its possession for 150 years, give or take."

Jean-Paul and Sara looked at each other, both wearing the same shocked expression. "How...how is this possible?" Sara pleaded with the elder priest, trying to wrap her head around the situation.

"Time travel?" the Monsignor replied, shaking his head. "I couldn't begin to tell you. This isn't like *Back to the Future* where you get into your DeLorean, press a few buttons and *ZOOP!* you're in the past."

"So, what? Like, a wormhole then?" Jean-Paul offered.

"Maybe?" the Monsignor replied, shrugging.

Sara sank into her chair. "I...I don't understand."

"Well, our current theoretical understanding of wormholes is that they are tunnels that link two points in spacetime; either two different points in space at the same time, the same point in space at two different times, or both," the Monsignor explained, gesturing in the air with his hands to illustrate what he was describing.

"So, you're talking about a wormhole that links the same point in space at two different times?" Jean-Paul asked. He was trying his best to sound like he was following the insane conversation.

"No, that won't quite do it," Father Julien interjected.

The Monsignor continued. "Relativity suggests that points in spacetime are independent of the matter that occupies it. You see the chair you're sitting on? Right now it's occupying a specific point in spacetime. But remember, the Earth is spinning on its axis, while it rotates around our sun, while the sun moves through the galaxy dragging the planets along with it. In a moment, your chair will be thousands of kilometres away from where it is right now. If you created a wormhole that connected right here, right now to where that chair was two minutes ago and stepped through it you'd likely be walking into the vacuum of space. If this is a wormhole, it would have to be one that somehow connects the same place on Earth between two different times, regardless of where the Earth is in the universe."

"I think I'm following you...but what could do that?" Jean-Paul asked.

The Monsignor shrugged as the other priests raised their eyebrows. "That's the million-dollar question. Whatever...or whoever did this is...it is nothing short of incredible. We may be witnessing a previously unseen natural phenomenon, a technology beyond our comprehension, or... a modern miracle of God's will."

"Okay...hold it," Sara said, sitting up and raising her hands. "None of this is making sense and I want to get back to the issue at hand.

You said you've had my husband's cell phone for 150 years. Why didn't you do anything to stop him from going on his hike?"

"Well, we didn't actually know it was a cell phone until a few days ago," Father Nic replied.

"And we only got the data off it this morning," Father Julien reminded her.

"And...in a way...your husband asked us not to," the Monsignor added.

"What?" Sara said in response. Her confusion and frustration were visibly mounting.

The Monsignor raised his hands in an effort to calm her down and spoke firmly. "I think it will become clearer if we continue."

Sara shook her head in bewilderment as the group turned back to look at the screen as the next video started.

"Okay...I'm not insane. I'm actually seeing this. So what is going on here? Is this like *Journey to the Center of the Earth*? Did I fall into a sinkhole and end up deep underground? No. The constellations are still there at night. So if I'm seeing mammoths the only other explanation is that I've somehow travelled back in time...like ten thousand years. In fact...I think I never even moved physically. I appeared at the Upland Cave reserve exactly as it was in the past, except here in this time it's underwater! That's why I didn't drown when I blacked out because I never actually blacked out. It also explains why my phone says that it's May 19th at 8pm when it's clearly earlier in spring and the middle of the day!"

Jake's face lit up in realization. "This explains everything! That's why there are so many animals and birds! That's why I'm seeing goddamned woolly mammoths! That's why I haven't seen any airplanes, satellites, or any signs of civilization! Because for me..."

Jake paused, the colour draining from his face as the reality of his situation sank in. "...because for me," he said slowly and quietly, "none of that exists yet".

He slid his backpack off, dropping it to the ground, then fell to his knees, staring off into space. "There's nobody looking for me because there is nobody out there. Sara...sh-she doesn't even know I'm missing yet because it's not going to happen for thousands of years. Hell, she doesn't even exist yet."

Jake swallowed hard, sniffled, and wiped a tear away from his eye. "I...I don't know why I'm even recording this. Nobody's ever going to see it."

He broke down, crying. He reached his hand to the screen and the playback ended.

"Oh my God," Sara said, as she broke down crying as well. "Was that it? Please tell me there's more."

The Monsignor put his hand gently on her shoulder. "Yes. There's more." He looked over at Father Julien who advanced to the next video.

Jake's face appeared, his eyes swollen and red from crying. He was sitting on the ground in the shade of a tree. He sniffled and wiped his nose with his sleeve before speaking.

"So I gotta say that I've pretty down the past several hours. It's hard to accept the fact that I'm going to die before I was even born...hell, before my great-great-great-great-great-whatever grandfather was born! And the thought of never seeing Sara, or Darren, or any of my family again...I gotta tell you that I did think that maybe it'd be better off if I were dead."

He looked off to the side as he regained his composure. "But I don't think I could ever actually kill myself. And when I thought about it some more...all of this is...a gift. Think about it: I'm the first person in ten thousand years to see a woolly mammoth! I played *If I Had a Million Dollars* by The Barenaked Ladies from my phone's playlist a little while ago and I am technically the first person on Earth to ever hear that song! Hell, I might be the first human who ever set foot in this part of Manitoba!"

The sound of a mastodon trumpeting nearby interrupted his soliloquy.

"I wonder if I'm the first person to travel through time? I'm not even sure how it happened, but if it was some kind of accident or natural occurrence maybe it's happened to other people, too. Maybe that explains mysterious disappearances throughout history? Like

Bermuda Triangle stuff? Though I guess what I need to think about now is what my next move should be."

Jake ended the recording.

Without prompting, Father Julien resumed the slideshow. The next thirty or so files were pictures of the mastodon herd that Jake had taken from a variety of angles from along the treeline. There were a few photos of a campsite he had made; a simple lean-to next to a fire pit encircled by rocks. He had taken panorama shots of the area showing dozens of the giant beasts, along with modern-looking deer grazing alongside them. In the western horizon beyond the prairie was the dark treeline of more forest.

Finally the slideshow arrived at the first frame of the next video. Jake's face once again filled the screen, but his beard now showed several days more growth. Father Julien started the playback which shuddered into action as Jake was once again walking as he recorded.

"My phone died while I was taking photos of the herd and it was cloudy for a few days so I couldn't recharge it until today. It took most of the morning to get it charged enough to record a video. I've camped a few days alongside them and just watched them. They're fascinating creatures. I've also found out they're not afraid of me, so I can move among them and as long as I keep my distance from the babies they're fine. See?"

Jake stopped walking and turned the camera. Two large mastodons appeared in the scene about twelve feet away. As if on cue, they grunted. Turning the camera back onto himself, he started walking away from the pair, glancing up every few moments to keep an eye on them and the other beasts around him. Once he was at a safer distance Jake's smile fell and his face grew more pensive.

"So I've had some time to think about things. Thanks to some basic history lessons, my Intro to Geology course at U of M, the interpretive centre at Oak Hammock Marsh, and late-night Wikipedia deep dives I have a better idea of what's going on. I'm also pretty positive that my gut feeling was right, and I'm still in Manitoba. Allow me to explain!"

Jake raised his free arm and stretched it out, spinning slowly as he continued, creating a bit of a dizzying panorama that made the Monsignor put his hand to his stomach and look away from the screen.

"Almost all of Canada was under a glacier until the start of the current geological period of warming called the Holocene. That was about ten or twelve thousand years ago. As the glaciers receded most of Manitoba was covered by a giant lake called Lake Agassiz which gradually drained away into Hudson's Bay, leaving behind Lake Winnipeg, Lake Manitoba, and all the thousands of other lakes here. I'm pretty sure I actually am somewhere near Cedar Lake, though obviously a few centuries after Aggasiz had receded quite a bit. The trees and plants are almost exactly like what we have in Manitoba back in 2019."

Jake continued walking as he lectured. "Given the fact that the animals here don't seem afraid of me I'm guessing they haven't seen any humans yet".

He furrowed his brow. "But if the first Native Americans came across the Bering Strait land bridge 13,000 years ago there should be some in North America by now...but who knows? Maybe they're here and they haven't come this far inland yet."

He shook his head and resumed his original train of thought. "Anyhow, I've decided I'm going to try and survive. My big problem is that I don't have a lot of supplies, and given that this is still likely Manitoba, even if I survive the summer I probably won't be able to survive the winter. I may be at the tail end of it, but it's still an ice age. And besides, humans are social creatures; we're not meant to be alone.

"So here's my plan: I'm heading south, just like before. The first Native Americans have to be on the continent; they just probably haven't come this far west or this far north in Manitoba, yet. Either way, the further south I go, the better chance I have of surviving the winter and the better chance I have of finding other people. I've also decided to start recording myself again because if by some miracle I make it back to my own time I'm going to need proof that this wasn't all some crazy dream. That, and I think I'll go crazy if I don't talk to someone other than myself.

He smirked at the camera and the playback ended.

Father Julien immediately switched to the next video and hit the play button, which displayed a large creek flowing quickly. The sound of the water was loud, and Jake was shouting offscreen to be heard over it.

"Check this out! So Sara loves to scroll through random videos on her phone all day, ok? And one time I was watching over her shoulder and there was this survival video of a couple lost in the wilderness without any tools or supplies. They used reeds to fashion a funnel-like cage that is tapered at one end and open wide at the other. They put it in a stream wedged between some rocks and waited and eventually a large fish swam into it thinking it was a safe space. Then they simply scooped it up out of the water and *voila*! They've got a fish that they cook up over the fire and eat straight up. So watch this!"

He moved towards some rocks in the stream where he gestured to a funnel-shaped object fashioned out of sticks and prairie grasses similar to the one he described. He pulled it up out of the water, carried it a few feet back up the bank and dumped it. A small big-mouth bass fell out and started flopping in the grass.

"Ha ha!" Jake hollered triumphantly. "Thank you pointless Facebook videos! Today I eat like a king!" The video ended.

"I remember that survival video," Sara said to the group, half chuckling, half sobbing. "I thought it was stupid."

The next video was clearly taken at night, with a campfire illuminating his face and crackling noisily in the background.

"I caught two more fish today, which I had for dinner. They were quite good, and I had berries and the last of my rations for dessert. I've left the trap out overnight, and assuming I have a fish or two in the morning I'll cook them up and bring them with me. I should probably figure out how to smoke fish so that they'll have a longer shelf life. You know, I regret never learning how to hunt or fish like Darren, but it's not like those were skills needed to survive in the twenty-first century."

A loud snap was heard and Jake looked around nervously before facing the camera again. He lowered his voice.

"Back when I was with the mammoths I noticed that while they kept an eye on me some of the time they kept looking off to the treeline in the distance. I think there was something out there watching them. I heard what sounded like howling a few of the nights I spent with them. I'm guessing wolves. Over the last couple of days though, I think they've been getting closer to me. I'm going to keep the fire going strong tonight just to make sure nothing decides to come at me."

Jake reached over and picked up a long stick with a sharpened end and showed it to the camera.

"I was using this as a walking stick but I decided to start sharpening the tip just in case I run into anything unpleasant. I guess if I'm in the stone age I should start acting like it!" He chuckled as he reached out and stopped the recording.

The next video had been shot again at night, and Jake's facial expression was one of fear. He spoke rapidly, his voice just above a whisper. "The battery is just about dead, but they've definitely been tracking me! I still haven't seen them but they're really close tonight! Listen!"

A few moments passed and all that was heard was the crackling of the campfire. Suddenly a hauntingly low howling sound started quietly and grew louder, rising in pitch. A second one joined it, followed by a third, and a fourth. The eerie chord filled the room until it gradually died away.

"That's not like any wolfsong I've ever heard bef—" Jake started to say before the video abruptly ended.

"What the hell was that?!" exclaimed Jean-Paul.

Father Nic chimed in. "We sent the audio to the Pontifical Academy of Sciences' zoology experts a few hours before you arrived. Their preliminary report was that it was canine, but it matched no known breed of dog or wolf."

"Are we really holding this up so we can talk about dog noises?" Sara said impatiently.

"Of course. My pardons, *Signora*," the Monsignor said, and they turned their attention back to the screen.

The next video was once again of Jake walking through a forested area. His face was dirty and his hair and beard were dishevelled. The solar panel array was sitting on the brim of his hat, reflecting the sunlight as he moved. "I walked through a couple of streams and travelled downwind to try and throw them off my scent and I think it worked. I haven't heard them for a day or two. It's been pretty cloudy so it's taken a while for me to get the phone charged up enough to record again. I've managed to rig the solar charger to my hat so the phone can keep charging while I'm on the move. Really glad I brought the six foot USB cable with me."

He swung the phone around so it was pointing ahead of him. The trees were a mix of conifer and birch, and ferns were starting to sprout from the ground. "Another plus is that it feels like it's getting warmer each day," he said as he filmed the path ahead of him. "Though what's weird is that normally I get sunburned really easily because I'm so pale. I didn't bring any sunblock with me on this trip because it's only late spring and we weren't going to be out for very long. But I've gotten way more sunlight with all this walking than I normally do and I haven't burned at all. Maybe the ozone layer is thicker in this time or something?

"Assuming the clock on my phone is still keeping time accurately, I've been here for almost three weeks and at the rate I'm moving I must have covered somewhere between one hundred and three hundred kilometres. I don't know where the Red River is exactly, if it even exists yet, but I figure as long as I head due south I'll eventually hit the Assiniboine River and maybe follow it east to The Forks. Hopefully it'll be a landmark I can recognize." He stopped the recording.

The next items in the slideshow were photographs Jake took of the scenery. Small creeks, grassy clearings, tiger lilies, and crocuses. A few photos of deer, a variety of birds, insects including strange-looking grasshoppers, and a small group of extremely large bison, which Father Nic identified as *Bison antiquus*, who had been thought to have already been extinct but had clearly survived another thousand years in isolated groups in the area. These giant creatures clearly had no contact with humans yet, as Jake was brave enough to take some selfies dangerously close to the massive herbivores. They towered almost a metre above Jake. Several other photos were of garter snakes.

"Weird that he photographed those so close up," Sara said to the group. "Jake really doesn't like snakes."

When the next video started, Jake's face filled the frame as usual. "So I'm just walking along here, minding my own business, and look what I come across..."

He swung the camera around. Initially the image was out of focus and the ground appeared to be moving. As it came into focus it revealed that the ground ahead was in fact covered in thousands of writhing garter snakes.

"That's right...snakes! Why did it have to be snakes? Oh! Oh! How about 'I have had it with these motherfucking snakes on this motherfucking plain'? But plain as in P-L-A-I-N? Does that work better?"

He laughed, then turned the camera back on himself. "Seriously, though. It's going to be a pain in the ass to get through these guys. Garter snakes aren't poisonous, but I think they can still bite. I'll try to use my walking stick here to 'encourage' them to stay out of my way...hey! I wonder if I'm near that place...oh, what's-it-called...Narcissist or something like that. The place with all the garter snakes! I went on a couple of field trips to it back when I was in grade school."

He peered closely at the phone. "Battery's almost dead and there isn't much sunlight right now. That's okay, though. I think it's best if I have both hands free while I walk through the valley of snakes here. I'll record more once I have some juice." He touched the screen, ending the recording.

"Narcissist?" the Monsignor asked.

Jean-Paul explained. "I think he means Narcisse. It's a place in Manitoba renowned for having a huge garter snake population."

"Oh, right. Duh," Sara said in a self-deprecating fashion. "I think I was there a couple times as a kid."

When the next video was queued up, the initial frame showed Jake with a big smile on his face. On his hat was the solar charging panel with the wire running down behind his back. Sara and Jean-Paul lit up in surprise at the change in his demeanour. When the playback started his smile grew even wider.

"Guess what?" Jake rhetorically asked into the camera. "For the first time in weeks I think I know where I am!" He pointed the camera down to show he was high in the branches of a large maple tree with forest behind him. Then he turned it away from his face and lifted the camera upwards. Ahead of him, bushes and shrubs gave way to bullrushes, reeds, and swamp as far as the eye could see, with small grassy hills poking up in the landscape. Massive flocks of birds could be seen taking off and landing against the clear blue sky. The lab was filled with a cacophony of birdsong, the calls of waterfowl, and frogs croaking. He held the camera there for a minute before turning it back on himself.

His eyes rolled up as he searched his memory. "If I remember the tour guide from Oak Hammock Marsh correctly, let's see...before European settlers arrived and drained the wetlands to make farmland, the marsh extended all the way from Winnipeg to...I think it was Teulon. I think I'm somewhere in that area. And I know, I know...that's not terribly interesting or helpful. But this is:"

He turned the camera back towards the horizon and then zoomed in. Far in the distance a large mound rose up, just perceptible above the tops of the reeds and marsh plants. "I think that's Stony Mountain! It has to be! It's the only elevated terrain anywhere near the marsh. That's where they'll build the prison in the 1800's."

Jake turned the camera back to face himself and brought a scratched and muddy hand up to wipe away a tear that was running down his cheek. "I know I'm thousands of years from home and it's dumb to get emotional, but God damn it I'm so happy to see something I recognize!"

He took a few moments to compose himself. "There aren't that many big trees here in the marsh so I'm going to head to Stony Mountain. That should give me a better view of the surrounding land and help me choose where to go next."

Suddenly Jake looked off into the distance and leaned forward, squinting. "What the hell is that...holy shit!" he exclaimed as his ears went wide. He glanced down at the phone and turned it back towards the marsh. The scene was blurred from the motion as he moved it back and forth, causing the Monsignor to groan quietly, until he had located what he had seen. As the camera came into focus a large brown mound could be seen sticking out of the water a few hundred metres into the marsh. To everyone in the room's surprise the mound started to move until it reached the bank on the right. As it left the water it became obvious it was a beaver but at the distance it was being viewed it was clearly the size of a bear.

"*Castoroides*," Father Nic explained to the group, his eyes not leaving the screen. "A giant beaver that is obviously now extinct."

Jake kept the camera on the massive beaver until it waddled off into the thick grasses. "It's late afternoon right now so I'm going to set up camp here and rest until tomorrow. And I think it'd be a good idea if I steer clear of those things," he spoke with an apprehensive tone as the video came to an end.

The next several dozen files were photos of the marsh as he started making his way towards Stony Mountain. Closeups of large butterflies and dragonflies, various small marsh birds, and cranes and herons of all species and sizes, including large groups of what the priests identified as whooping cranes. There were a few photos of garter snakes and a couple of other types of snakes that the priests couldn't identify. Every once in a while, he had taken a shot of the escarpment along the southern horizon, showing that it was getting larger as he got closer.

Jake would occasionally reach small hills protruding from the marsh and would take videos where he simply panned the camera over the scenery. The sound of millions of birds calling, insects buzzing, and frogs croaking was deafening. He had a few videos where he was only a few dozen metres from some of the giant beavers swimming in the marsh.

Jake didn't speak during any of those videos; he didn't need to. These images and videos were a welcome departure from the panic and gloom that had dominated the recordings up until this point, and Jean-Paul almost felt like he was looking at someone's vacation photos on Facebook.

That all changed when the first frame of a video came up showing Jake's face with a look of worry. When Father Julien pressed play the scene came to life with Jake panting heavily. "It's taken me longer to get to Stony Mountain than I thought. Probably because I can't exactly go in a straight line and I've been trying my best to avoid deep water and muddy parts of the swamp. But that's not my biggest problem today."

He pointed the camera north, the direction in which he had come from, in a view overlooking the marsh. He was standing in waist-high grass on top of a small mound a few feet higher than the surrounding bog. As he held the camera steady his free hand came into view pointing off into the distance. "There!" he shouted.

"I don't see anything," Sara said. Father Julien pressed a few keys to rewind as Father Nic stood up and walked over to the projector screen. When the playback resumed he pointed to an area of tall grass in the distance, where a few dark objects could be seen darting along the bank of a section of the marsh. Once again Jake's hand came into view pointing at the spot and he shouted. As they watched the objects darted in and out of the grass again. Jake turned the camera back to face him.

"I'm pretty sure those are the wolf things from last week. I think they picked up my scent again and are stalking me. This isn't good. There's definitely more than two out there. And like everything else in this time, they're big."

He swung the camera around and pointed it towards the southwest. Not too far from his location was a stony outcrop overlooking a small area covered with gravel and sparse vegetation. "I'm going to set up there tonight. It'll be good shelter and once I get a fire going it'll hopefully keep them away".

Once again he pointed the camera at his face and swallowed hard. "I have a bad feeling about this." He shook his head as the video came to an end.

The next video queued was frozen on a black picture. Before Father Julien could start playback, the Monsignor raised his hand at him to wait, and turned towards Sara.

"*Signora* Taylor, I feel I must warn you that this next video is unsettling."

Sara's face blanched and she swallowed hard, nodding her head in approval rapidly. "It's okay," she said quietly. "I can watch this".

The Monsignor turned his head and nodded at Father Julien to proceed.

The black video screen was revealed to be a video taken at night. The camera was pointed at a campfire and then swung around to reveal a terrified Jake, his face half in shadow, the other half dimly coloured orange from the flickering firelight. He spoke in a hushed tone. "The wolves are here. I've tried making noise, throwing rocks, but they're in the brush just beyond the firelight and they aren't leaving."

He directed the camera towards the deer grass and bushes at the end of the gravel bed where he was camped out. The dancing firelight caused shadows to play across the branches making the whole scene look like hundreds of writhing creatures. In addition to the crackling fire was the sound of several creatures moving through the brush. Several times the reflection of green eyes would appear peering through the grass and then vanish.

He held the phone away from his body to get a better selfie view of himself. In his left hand was his sharpened walking stick. The fear could be seen in his face. "I've tried to make a basic weapon here, but I don't know if I'll be able to hold them all—"

Without warning a huge, blurred figure flew into the scene and bright white teeth clamped down on his left forearm. Jake screamed out in pain and the phone was thrown from his hands, landing several feet away. The wolves had made the first move.

By pure fortune the camera still pointed in Jake's direction. Above the outcrop behind Jake was the moon, captured by the phone as a fuzzy white dot. Between the moonlight and the firelight Jake could be seen thrashing on the ground as he wrestled with the massive animal who had him by the arm. Even in the dim light, the crimson red of Jake's blood was visible where the wolf was biting. Jake yelled, kicked, and punched at the creature but it would not let him go. Two other large wolves moved into the scene and encircled the battling duo, looking for a spot to strike. When the light caught their faces their eyes lit up green and their snarling visages revealed glistening white fangs.

"Oh God," Sara cried out, bringing her hand to her mouth. The Monsignor put a hand on her shoulder.

At that moment a large figure appeared on the outcrop, blocking out the moon. Before the camera could refocus it flew down from the outcrop emitting a terrifying scream and landed on the ground next to Jake, striking the wolf that was upon him. The wolf let go of Jake as it yelped and backed away snarling. The other two wolves leapt back in fear and retreated off-camera. The camera finally refocused and nobody in the room watching needed to be told what they were seeing; a sabre-toothed cat.

Jake was moaning as the giant cat growled at the wolf and jumped at it, immediately catching the wolf's neck in its jaws and dragging it to the ground. There was a sickening sound of bones crunching, at which point the wolf silently flopped down and remained motionless, its neck broken. The other wolves yelped out menacingly from off screen but their cries grew fainter as they retreated back into the brush.

At this point Jake had seen the fearsome cat and started backing away from the feline and its kill, clumsily sliding along the ground back towards the camera.

"Oh shit! Oh shit! Oh shit!" he muttered.

The cat seemed to ignore Jake and, satisfied that the wolf was dead, picked it up by its neck and dragged it into the brush and off camera. Out of immediate danger, Jake dropped flat onto his back. The sounds of moving grass and snapping branches faded away, followed by a silence broken only by the occasional pop from the campfire. Eventually crickets nearby started chirping again to accompany the sound of Sara weeping softly in the lab.

Stunned, Jake laid there for a few minutes holding his bleeding left arm with his right hand. Only the slow rising and falling of his stomach in the dim light gave any indication to the group watching the video that he was still alive. Gradually he rolled onto his right side, trying to get a look at the injury in the firelight. Looking around, he noticed the phone that was still filming him. He absentmindedly started to reach with his left arm and cried out in pain as blood could be seen dripping onto the gravel in front of him. He rolled onto his back and blindly reached out with his right hand until it connected with the phone. The scene shuddered and shook as he groped at the phone, finally grasping it in his hands and raising it above his head, bringing his face into view. Even in the dim light he looked ashen and a small trickle of blood ran from the corner of his mouth.

"I think I'm in shock," he panted. "I'm going to get back to the fire, see if I can bandage this wound, and hopefully I don't die from blood loss," he said. The camera shook as he fumbled with one hand to stop the recording.

"Jesus," Jean-Paul muttered, breaking the silence of the room. He then looked at the three priests in the room and sheepishly muttered "Sorry".

"It's ok," the Monsignor said as he produced a hip flask, opened it, and took a swig. He offered it to Jean-Paul and Sara, both of whom declined.

Father Nic produced his tablet once again to show them reconstructions of a creature called the dire wolf. It was a large species of wolf that went extinct along with the rest of the megafauna at the start of the Holocene. Ironically, an artistic recreation from the early twentieth century illustrated a dire wolf squaring off against a smilodon, or what is commonly known as a sabre-toothed cat.

"Was that the last video?" Sara asked timidly after Nic took the tablet back.

The Monsignor gave a hopeful, tight-lipped smile. "No, *Signora*. By the grace of God, no."

At that Father Julien advanced to the next video and started it. It was daytime and Jake's face looked gaunt. "I managed to stop the bleeding last night while I was still in shock. I must have passed out pretty hard afterwards because it was well into the afternoon before I woke up. I guess those damn wolves are gone, as is that fucking sabre-toothed cat. Thank God."

He pointed the camera at a piece of blood-soaked fabric wrapped around his left arm. "I think I got the bleeding stopped, and I've taken the rest of the drugs in my pack for the pain. They're not really effective as they're just over-the-counter painkillers, but I'm more worried about how I don't have anything to disinfect a wound this size. I also don't have access to any antibiotics in case that thing's bite infected me with anything. But that's not even the worst of it..."

Jake slowly walked over to his backpack, and pointed the camera at it. Jean-Paul and Sara stared hard to make out the tan object sitting on top of it before he got close for them to recognize it as Jake's hat, with the solar charging panel affixed. The panel was snapped in half. Sara gasped in realization before Jean-Paul understood the significance.

"One of those bastards stepped on it, or it happened when it was knocked off. Either way, it's not producing any electricity any more and I can't fix it."

He swung the camera back towards his blood and mud-stained face. "Without the panel there's no electricity and my phone was only at 60% when I was attacked last night. It's at 53% right now."

He sat down on the ground, wincing as he did, the outcrop visible behind him. He wiped sweat away from his forehead with his good hand which was holding the phone, causing the picture to violently jerk with his movements before he settled it back down to point at his face.

His voice broke as a tear rolled down his cheek. "Once this charge is done, I can't take any more videos or photos. I also won't be able to look at Sara any more." Shifting from sadness to anger he cried out. "This was my last tangible connection to home...damn it!"

He sat for a minute or so staring off in the distance and breathing heavily. Finally he looked back into the camera. "My best bet is still Stony Mountain," he continued, trying to sound courageous through the tears. "If I can get there...if there are any humans around...they might be able to help. I've got to conserve the battery," he said as he stopped the recording.

Father Julien advanced to the next video and pressed play. Jake's face once again filled the screen, but was somehow more pale than the last video. Behind him were branches and leaves.

"So it turns out I was only about seven or eight hours away from Stony Mountain. I've spent the night here and I wanted to show you this." He turned the camera and slowly panned it in a full circle, capturing a panorama of the surrounding environment. He was several metres above the marsh on a rocky outcrop overgrown with brush and small trees. He had climbed a larger oak, which provided an amazing vantage point.

He narrated as he panned, his voice laboured. "To the north and east is the marsh."

At the eastern horizon a winding treeline heading south could be seen. "I'll bet that's the Red River, or whatever will become it".

As he faced due south he paused. "In my time, I'd be able to see the skyline of downtown Winnipeg from here, and all the farmland in between. But look at this...pure, virgin territory. This...is what my home looked like before people."

Stretching south before him were the last remnants of the marsh as it transitioned into a large, open grassland with clusters of bush and large stones left behind centuries previous by the retreating glacier. No buildings, roads, or high-tension power lines from the northern dams interrupted the scene. Instead there were large herds of animals. They were too far away to make out but they were likely giant bison, deer, and mastodon. Jean-Paul had travelled through that region many times in his lifetime, past the giant penitentiary on the hill where Jake now stood, and he marvelled at how different and how beautiful the area was.

The terrain in the distance to the north-east was much rockier. He pointed at it. "Just past there must be where Stonewall, Manitoba will be founded".

He continued panning, pausing for a moment to focus on a small group of deer running along the edge of the marsh. Jake chuckled.

"Ten thousand years in the past, surrounded by creatures no human has seen in millenia, and I stop to shoot white-tailed deer!"

He completed his panorama and turned the camera back to himself. "I've been watching for a few hours now," he said as the light-heartedness of the previous moment faded into a grim look on his face. "And I've seen no smoke from campfires or anything else that would suggest a human presence."

He looked down and dropped from the tree to the ground, the scene becoming blurry as he fell and crouched upon landing. Staying crouched, he steadied the phone and lowered his voice.

"There's another problem now, too. I've started to get cold. It's a warm day which means this is the onset of chills. Fever will follow. This means I've gotten an infection from the attack. It's not surprising, given that a modern human like me isn't likely going to have any natural immunities to the bacteria in prehistoric monster wolf mouths."

Jake stood up, the large branch of the oak he had been standing on now appearing behind him just below his shoulders. He cleared his throat. "I have an idea though. But I'm going to stop recording and shut off my phone to save battery power for now. I'll fill you in when I'm done."

The video ended.

The Monsignor motioned for Father Julien to wait and turned to Sara and Jean-Paul. "This next video...it is the last file we retrieved from the phone."

"Oh God," Sara blurted out, choking on her words. Both Jean-Paul and the Monsignor placed a hand on each shoulder to support her but she nodded that she was okay to continue. Jean-Paul removed his hand, but the Monsignor let his hand remain in place as he turned to nod at Father Julien. Father Julien started the final clip.

Jake's face came into the scene, even more pale than before and dripping with sweat. "Okay," he said slowly, his voice raspy. "It's been a few days since the last video and I've been getting worse. I've had chills, fever, puking and diarrhea, and now a cough."

As if on cue, he was suddenly overcome with a brief coughing fit. "I've never been this sick in my life. I don't think I'm making it off Stony Mountain. But I'll show you what I've managed to do."

He turned the phone to point at a large pile of rocks, a cairn, placed in a basic four-sided pyramid shape with a flat top and simple *inukshuk* on the plateau. In the centre of the cairn was a cavity. He pointed the camera down in front of the pile where two roughly rectangular blocks of mud lay.

Jake had another short coughing fit before he could start speaking. "I was thinking about movies like *Back to the Future*. When messages had to be sent from one person in the past to another in the future, as long as the message survived it'd appear instantly for the recipient. So I figured the best message I can send is my phone. In an hour or so it'll be dead and useless to me. The problem of course, is that there's no Western Union here to hold on to and deliver the phone for me in 2019. So how do I ensure that a phone will survive ten thousand years?"

He crouched, bringing the camera close up to the mud blocks. The one on the left had an indentation that looked slightly larger than a cell phone. The one on the right was decorated with shells and colourful rocks, and the letters "INRI" were scratched deep into the surface at the top along with "OPEN ON 2019-05-17" across the bottom.

"I've read stories of toads being found alive encased in solid clay. And things like the Dead Sea Scrolls survived over a thousand years by being kept out of the elements. So I'm making a clay brick here that I've decorated and dried out as best I can in my fire. I'm going to wrap the phone in as much plastic as I have and seal it in the brick. Then I'm placing the brick in the hole here in this cairn and then filling it in with dirt and rocks."

Jake turned the phone back to his face as he slowly sat on the ground, a pained look crossing his face as he did so. "The plastic is to keep the moisture out of the phone. Sealing it in a mud brick should help keep extreme temperature changes from the plastic, and protect it from being crushed or invaded by insects and animals. Now if it survives, there are two groups of people that might eventually find this: the First Nations, which will be a tribe like the Cree or Ojibwe, and then the Europeans who will settle this area in the 1800s. The *inukshuk* is for the first group. In my time, the First Nations respect stone artwork by their ancestors and I'm hoping that's a tradition that was handed down from the people of this time. So when the first people get here they'll see the cairn and *inukshuk* and attribute it to ancestors, spirits, gods, or whatever, and leave it alone."

Jake reached off camera with his injured left arm, wincing as he brought the engraved top half of the brick into view. "This bit is for the Europeans. I can't have someone finding my phone before the year 2019 and screwing up history, so just like with the First Nations, I'm going to bank on European superstition. I've carved the Christian fish symbol, a cross, and the letters INRI which decorate a lot of crucifixes. That should make it clear to any European that this is a religious artefact. I remember watching a documentary on some kids from Fatima who claimed to have seen the Virgin Mary and received secrets from her, and they turned the secrets over to the Church with instructions that they couldn't be revealed until the future. Apparently the Church respected those wishes. Hopefully the 'OPEN ON' date here will make them think it contains a prophecy about the future. Since the first settlers here are mostly Roman Catholics, odds are if it survives the Church will find it and keep it safe, just like with Fatima."

Jake put the brick back down. "Now, if you're watching this, you're probably wondering why I'm telling them to open the brick after the date I went back in time. I've thought a lot about this. If I let them open it just a few weeks before I left, maybe they could stop me...but what if that causes some sort of paradox and destroys the universe? And despite the fact that I think I'm dying...I'm okay with it. I've seen so much...more than I probably should have ever seen. This has been a gift and I don't think I should throw it away. So I decided to mark it for opening ten days after I came back here. Why ten days? After all, my phone says that it's June 16th today, so why not today's date? I couldn't really decide what was best, but I figure ten is a nice, round number."

Jake coughed some more and the camera shook with each cough. "In a way, I'm lucky I got sick here on Stony. If I was healthy enough to make it I might have picked a spot like The Forks, but I have no idea if and where the Red and Assiniboine rivers meet in this time. My geology course taught me that rivers change a lot over eons and odds are where they are today isn't where they'll be in 2019. Also, the Red River Valley is a massive floodplain, so building anything at ground level will likely get destroyed over thousands of years of flooding. This high ground gives my phone its best odds."

Jake paused to catch his breath, growing visibly weaker, and a tear ran down his cheek. "I-I don't know if there's a God, but if by some miracle this phone survives to 2019, it will at least give Sara and Darren some closure."

He closed his eyes, and apparently overcome by exhaustion and illness he began to ramble. "Maybe this idea is crazy...it's probably crazy. Hell, I'm probably mad from this fever...last night I dreamed of fireworks..."

The video glitched for a moment, and Jake stopped talking. He brought the camera closer to his face and looked at the top corner of the screen with utter dismay. "5% battery. The phone is warning me that it's about to shut down."

He paused for a moment to breathe heavily, holding back tears. "If it's all the same to you, I'm going to use the last few minutes of battery life to look at a photo of Sara. It'll be the last time I see her. Then I'll bury this phone."

He pulled the camera back from face and looked into the screen. "Goodbye, Sara. I love you. I know we said we'd face whatever may come together, and I'm sorry I didn't hold up my end of the bargain. Please tell Darren that none of this was his fault."

He winced from pain as he brought his left hand up to his mouth to kiss his index and middle fingers then reached up and touched the screen. The video ended. Everyone sat in silence, save for Sara who wept quietly. All had tears streaming down their faces.

A few minutes passed, and the Monsignor nodded at Father Julien who pressed some buttons on the podium and turned the lights back on. Everyone winced and quickly grabbed tissues to wipe their noses.

"And now, the third and final story, though I'm sure you can guess most of it," the Monsignor began. As if on cue, Father Nic walked back into the adjoining room where he had gotten the cell phone pieces from earlier. The Monsignor leaned forward and rested his elbows on his knees, clasping his hands together.

"In 1870 European settlers started moving into the area now known as Stony Mountain, Manitoba. A man by the name of Isbister was one of the first settlers, and a team of European surveyors in his employ found a stone cairn overgrown with brush on the escarpment. The native guides accompanying the team refused to go near, citing superstitions and bad omens, but the surveying team dismantled the cairn regardless. No drawings or photos of it survive but we're sure it was the one that your husband built."

At that point Father Nic returned with another display case like the first. He set it down on the table and the Monsignor walked over to it. "This is what they found inside," the Monsignor continued, gesturing to the case.

Sara and Jean-Paul moved in closer. Inside the case were two halves of a roughly-formed brick of clay, just like the ones they had just seen in the video, but different. Older. The top half was on the left and was decorated with small stones of varying colour and a few cracked and broken snail shells. Still clearly visible were the letters "INRI" scratched across the top along with an ichthys, a cross, and the words "OPEN ON 2019-05-17" across the bottom. The bottom half of the clay brick was to the right, where one could clearly see the impression that the cell phone wrapped in plastic had left behind. Pieces of grass and water plants, used to hold the clay together, could be seen in the exposed interior.

Sara brought her hand up to her mouth. "Just like the video."

"When it was brought to Isbister's attention, he immediately took it to the nearest priest, who in turn brought it to Archbishop Taché at St. Boniface Cathedral in what is now Winnipeg. It was considered a holy artefact and was shipped to Rome under guard where it was placed in the Vatican Secret Archives."

"You've had this all along?" Sara asked, surprised.

"*Si*, though we had no idea what it was," the Monsignor responded. "Any artefacts that deal with prophecy are stored in a special section of the archives, and aside from superficial examination for record-keeping we are not permitted to open such objects until the date we are instructed to do so."

"This could still be a hoax of some kind," Jean-Paul countered. Sara gave him an incredulous look.

The Monsignor nodded approvingly. "I would be as sceptical as you, *Signor* Ducharme. However, this cannot be a hoax. You see, I started working as a young priest in the Vatican Secret Archives in 1979. I saw this artefact back then and recorded its presence in the paper inventories that have to be done every ten years. I also photographed it at that time. In 1983 I also logged the first digital record of it when we began switching over to computerized records."

The Monsignor walked over to one of the other tables and pulled a large, yellowed envelope off the surface and brought it over to the main examination table where the cases were. He opened the envelope and pulled out a large x-ray transparency. "In 1988 we had special dispensation from His Holiness John Paul II to x-ray the clay brick."

As he held up a transparency to the lights overhead, Jean-Paul and Sara adjusted in their seats to get a better viewing angle. Inside the ghostly outline of the clay brick was the slightly darker outline of the cell phone. The paths of the circuit board and some electrical components were unmistakable as bright white figures.

"From this x-ray we realized that we were looking at an electronic device more advanced than anything we had at the time, embedded in a clay brick which had been in the church's possession for over 100 years. Suffice it to say, we were very eager for May 17th, 2019 to arrive. I consider myself blessed that I lived to see that day."

He put down the x-rays and continued talking while Jean-Paul picked them up and examined them further. "On the 17th, we very carefully cut through the brick and extracted the phone. The plastic it was wrapped in had become very brittle and crumbled as we handled it. The entire process was documented on video with witnesses."

Father Nic produced a folder containing reports from a lab and showed it to Sara and Jean-Paul. "Samples of the organic material embedded in the clay were sent to three different labs for Carbon-14 testing. They all came back with dates of ten thousand years before present, plus-or-minus twelve hundred years."

The Monsignor resumed his explanation. "We spent several days carefully examining it and praying about how to proceed. But on the 22nd Father Julien decided to simply plug it in. Much to our shock, the screen came on indicating that the battery was charging. After letting it charge for a few minutes Father Julien decided to try and turn it on."

Father Julien grimaced sheepishly. "I guess even though it was sealed airtight, after ten thousand years it was likely that some of the capacitors had dried out, which is what caused the phone to finally die." He looked at Sara. "Not before it managed to send its coordinates to your phone, of course."

"Yes," the Monsignor sneered slightly at Father Julien. "Next time protocols will be completely observed."

"Next time?" Jean-Paul interjected, his eyes widening. "Are you saying you have more artefacts like this?"

"If only you kn—" Father Julien laughingly started before a stern glare from the Monsignor abruptly ended his statement.

Father Nic quickly changed the subject "The disk?" he said to Father Julien. The young priest disappeared into one of the adjoining rooms as Father Nic made a quiet phone call. Father Julien soon returned, holding out a jewel case containing an optical disc.

"This is a data DVD containing everything we extracted from your husband's phone," he said as he passed it to the Monsignor, who in turn held it out to Sara.

"Why are you giving this to me? Aren't you keeping all this a secret?" She reached out for it, but as she grasped it the Monsigner held on to his end of the case.

"The terms of the nondisclosure agreement you signed are still in effect," the Monsignor cautioned, glancing between the two. "If you attempt to go public with any of this the Church will disavow everything and you will be sued. However it is obvious that it was your husband's wish that we pass this information on to you and we are fulfilling that final request." He then let go of the case.

"Thank you," Sara said sincerely, placing it in her handbag. She wiped a tear from her cheek.

"You know, I feel a little bit like Joe Flaherty," the Monsignor chuckled, smiling at the two Canadians. Jean-Paul and Sara looked at each other, puzzled. The Monsignor furrowed his brow at their confusion.

"Joe Flaherty? Canadian actor? He was the Western Union man at the end of *Back to the Future II* who delivered the letter to Marty from Doc. It's like this is the same, except I'm delivering you these messages from Jacob."

Sara feigned recognition as she smiled and nodded.

"I saw that movie once or twice when I was a kid," Jean-Paul said, shrugging apologetically.

Father Nic hung up his phone and put it away. "I have just arranged a car to take you both wherever you need to go. It should be here momentarily."

They left the underground laboratory in silence. Following the Monsignor through the security doors and back up the musty stone staircase, they returned to the study. Fathers Nic and Julien immediately went to the globe to pour themselves drinks. The Monsignor went to his desk and picked up the framed photo of Jake, and he returned it to Sara.

When the car arrived, Sara and Jean-Paul bid the priests farewell, with Jean-Paul shaking their hands and Sara hugging each of them. When she got to Father Julien she hugged him the tightest.

"Thank you, most of all," she said quietly in his ear.

"For what, *Signora*?"

"For turning on the phone," she said, pulling back from him with a half smile through her tears.

"Ultimately we would have tried to find you and invite you here once it had been cleared with His Holiness," the Monsignor said. "After all, you were the intended recipient of *Signor* Taylor's messages. You just...what's the expression...beat us to the punch.

Father Nic then walked the Canadians back down the hall, opening the door and standing aside for them. Sara and Jean-Paul exited the building and stepped outside, immediately greeted with the cool air that follows a rainstorm. Water continued to pool and drip from the edges of the canopy over the door, but the rain was no longer falling.

"Thank you again," Sara said as she hugged him once more in the doorway.

Jean-Paul reached out and shook his hand. "Yeah...it's been...something."

"Indeed. I think words are going to fail us all on this subject for quite some time. This has been an amazing experience and my only regret is that we couldn't help you find your husband. I hope all this has provided some sort of closure."

"I honestly can't say...it sounds cliché, but I suppose time will tell."

Father Nic smiled softly. The driver of the car impatiently honked.

"I suppose we should be on our way," Jean-Paul said. Sara nodded in agreement.

"Goodbye, Father Nic."

"Safe journey, and may the Lord be with you," Father Nic said as he closed the door.

Sara and Jean-Paul each inhaled deeply, as if it had been their first opportunity to breathe that night. Turning their backs to the door the exhausted pair paid little attention to their surroundings as they shuffled in silence to the car. The driver held the door open as Sara, then Jean-Paul got into the back and sank into the seat. He looked over at Sara. She had sunk into her seat as he had and was sitting there with her purse on her lap and her hands on top of her purse, staring out her window. He thought about how different she looked now than in their first ride together.

Sara said little on the ride back to her hotel by the Rome Ciampino airport. When they arrived Jean-Paul had the driver wait while he saw her into the lobby. It was deserted at this hour, save for a young man asleep in his chair at reception. Sara turned to Jean-Paul as they reached the centre of the lobby.

"Are you staying in Rome at all?"

"No. I'm booking the first flight back to Winnipeg that I can get."

"Of course. What will you do now?"

"I'm not sure" Sara looked past Jean-Paul into the distance. "I just...need some time to process all this."

"Of course," Jean-Paul said, wincing in annoyance because he was repeating himself. "I can barely believe it myself and I saw everything you did."

He checked the time on this phone, the first time he had looked at it in hours. It was just before 4am.

"Is there anything else I can do?"

Sara's gaze returned to his face and her features softened. "Oh...no. No. Thank you so much, Jean-Paul!"

She gave a tight-lipped smile, stepped forward, and hugged him. "Thank you for everything you've done!"

"It was the least I could do," Jean-Paul said, half-returning the embrace. After Sara pulled away, he mimicked her grin and said "Well, good night. Safe journey!"

"Good night," Sara replied, and she turned and walked toward the staircase that led to the rooms.

"Wait," Jean-Paul called to her in a hushed tone. She turned back to face him.

"I...I just wanted to say...that I am very sorry for your loss. It feels weird to say it though because watching those videos made Jake seem very much alive...but I did want to give you my condolences."

Sara formed a tight-lip smile and nodded, as her eyes glistened. She gave a slight wave goodbye then started back towards the staircase.

Jean-Paul watched her start up the stairs then turned and left the hotel. Getting back into the car, he gave the driver the address of his flat and leaned back into the seat as they drove off, feeling as though this was the first time in days he could relax.

While riding in the car he pulled his phone out of his pocket and tried to look at it but found he couldn't focus on any of the information on the screen. He recalled how a few months ago he had dropped his phone from a small height and the screen had shattered, requiring him to get a replacement. As he studied it he marvelled at how fragile the device was, and yet somehow Jake's had survived for thousands of years encased in a brick of mud and grass.

Jake again. Here was a man who he knew nothing about a few hours ago but had now bore witness to the extraordinary last weeks of his life. Jean-Paul wondered about how he would feel in similar circumstances; dying alone in a strange place with literally no one on Earth to comfort him. He could envision only great loneliness and terror. How Jake was able to overcome it all and be almost optimistic about his situation was unfathomable. His plan to get a message to Sara over such a vast distance of time, despite all he had been through and the hopelessness of the situation, was incredible.

Trying to distract himself from his thoughts and the tears welling in his eyes he looked at his phone again and saw that it was just past 4am. He told himself he was happy it was a Saturday and that he didn't have to go in to work until Monday. Not that work felt like it meant anything at the moment.

By the time the car reached his flat, the last remnants of the rain clouds in the eastern sky were starting to glow pink and orange in anticipation of sunrise. Getting out of the car his nostrils were invaded by the smell of wet garbage in a public waste bin on the sidewalk. The city now seemed closed in compared to the infinite spaces Jake had photographed. It felt even more confining as he entered his building and marched up two narrow flights of stairs to his flat.

As he closed his door behind him, Jean-Paul kicked off his shoes and dropped his coat on the lone chair at his small kitchen table. Untying his necktie as he walked over to the bed, he dropped it on the floor. Without undressing any further he fell both into his bed and into a deep sleep.

In his dreams he found himself standing in a field back home in Manitoba. Looking up he saw blue skies stretching from horizon to horizon over unspoiled prairie and forest. All he could hear was the wind through the trees and the songs of the birds. As he walked through the waist-high grass and felt the warm sun on his skin, he looked ahead and saw Jake Taylor, smiling and taking a photo of a mastodon.

Chapter 3

Jean-Paul sat at his desk in the Canadian Consulate dealing with the usual paperwork that accompanied his position. It had been almost two weeks since he and Sara went to the secret lab in Vatican City and the experience had been all but pushed out of his mind by the consistent workload his job presented him with. His experience there and the incredible story of Jake Taylor's phone seemed like some surreal fading dream.

As his workday finished he signed the last of the documents on his desk and put them into his outbox. Logging out of his workstation and putting on his jacket, he bid good evening to his coworkers and walked over to the elevator. As he boarded he heard his supervisor Maria's voice call out "hold the lift!" so he pressed and held the "door open" button until she arrived.

As she got into the elevator with him she smiled at Jean-Paul and watched as he pressed the 'L' button for the lobby.

"Any plans this evening?" Maria asked him as the car lurched into its downward journey.

"No, probably just staying in," Jean-Paul admitted, shrugging. "You?"

"I'm on my way to pick up Antonella and we're doing an evening of fine dining and opera."

"Very nice."

Jean-Paul struggled to think of additional smalltalk. They both smiled at each other in silence as the elevator slowly made its way to the lobby. After what felt like an eternity the car jolted to a stop and the doors slid open.

"Have a good night," Jean-Paul said as he held the doors.

"You too," Maria replied as she exited the car.

He crossed the small lobby, exited the Consulate doors, and took the four small steps down to the sidewalk. He raised a hand to hail a taxi.

"*Signor* Ducharme!" someone called from across the street.

Jean-Paul looked over. Standing next to a black Renault was a Gendarme and the female Vatican lawyer from the previous Friday, the one Jean-Paul had Nicknamed "Frau Something-or-Other". Jean-Paul froze for a moment until she beckoned him over. He remembered at the last moment to quickly check for traffic before he crossed the narrow street.

"Yes?" Jean-Paul responded as he got closer.

"Monsignor Wowchuk has requested your presence," the lawyer said in a thick Italian accent.

He was taken aback slightly as he had been expecting her to sound German. Without waiting for Jean-Paul's reply, the Gendarme opened the rear passenger door.

Jean-Paul briefly considered protesting, but decided it would be pointless. So he loudly sighed, shook his head in disbelief and got into the back seat. The Gendarme closed the door behind him and got into the front. The lawyer joined Jean-Paul in the back.

"Can I ask what this is about? I didn't tell anyone anything, I swear."

The lawyer snorted dismissively in response and pulled out her phone, tapping away at it.

Rolling his eyes at her impoliteness, Jean-Paul leaned back into the seat and pulled his phone out of his breast pocket.

Before he could unlock his screen the lawyer snapped "No phones!"

He sighed again, put it away and awkwardly tried to rest his hands on his lap.

Despite being annoyed at the cloak-and-dagger nature of this journey, Jean-Paul didn't make any further attempts at talking. As the vehicle wound through the various streets and entered Vatican City, it became obvious where they were headed and soon they pulled up outside the same townhouse he and Sara were at before.

The Gendarme exited the car and opened the rear door for Jean-Paul. Stepping out of the vehicle, he could see the residence in the light of the early evening. Though the building had seemed foreboding at night, he was struck by how nondescript and uninteresting it was by day. The brown and gray brick of the walls and the old panes of glass in the windows were no different than any of the other buildings in the area. The awning which had shielded them from the rain was revealed to be a dull, sun-bleached purple, with tattered edges fluttering in the wind. Had the car not stopped directly in front of it, he would have had difficulty picking it out from any of the neighbouring units.

He briefly wondered if the other buildings on the block had secret passages to equally secret underground Vatican labs but his train of thought was derailed by the Gendarme ushering him away from the car. Jean-Paul stepped under the awning, approached the door and rang the bell, the lawyer waiting uncomfortably close behind him.

Father Nic opened the door and smiled upon seeing him. "*Signor* Ducharme! How good it is to see you again! Please come in! We've been expecting you."

The upbeat demeanour of the priest had caught Jean-Paul off guard as he stepped inside and wiped his feet on the mat. "I'm sorry, *padre*. Why exactly am I here?"

"You'll see, you'll see," he beckoned as he made his way down the hall to the study.

Jean-Paul and the lawyer followed after him. The windowless study was empty and seemed darker without a fire going in the fireplace. As soon as he entered the study the lawyer approached the Monsignor's desk, placed a briefcase on the surface and pulled out another NDA. It looked very much like the one Jean-Paul had signed the last time.

"Again?" Jean-Paul asked incredulously.

"Again," Father Nic said sternly, holding out a pen.

Once all documents were signed the lawyer produced a temporary badge as before, handed it to Jean-Paul, and left. Father Nic groped awkwardly until he found the release for the secret door under the desk. The bookcase popped open, and the two men proceeded to the hidden stairs. The familiar musty smell immediately filled Jean-Paul's nostrils.

Father Nic began walking down the stairs with Jean-Paul close behind. "What we weren't allowed to tell you the last time you were here was that there were other video files found on Stony Mountain in 1870."

"What?" Jean-Paul responded in shock, pausing briefly before looking back down as he descended the ancient staircase. "I don't understand."

"All will be explained in due time."

They passed through the short security hall and the musty smell of the passage was replaced with the hermetically-sealed air of the laboratory. Jean-Paul's ears popped as the door was closed behind them. Waiting for them was Father Julien and Monsignor Wowchuk.

"*Signor* Ducharme," the Monsignor said warmly as he clasped Jean-Paul's outstretched hand with both of his and shook it firmly. "It is good to see you again!"

"Likewise," Jean-Paul said hesitantly as he turned to shake Father Julien's hand. "But I'm surprised I'm here. Father Nic said there were more video files?"

"Indeed there was! We were not permitted to disclose their existence until today."

Jean-Paul looked around the otherwise empty room. "Is Sara here?"

"Protocol is very strict about this sort of thing," Father Nic chimed in. "We can't extend an invitation to *Signora* Taylor unless we know she's an intended recipient of the videos."

"Intended recipient? How am I a recipient and she's not?"

Father Julien gestured at the laptop on the podium. "We don't know…yet. These videos were encoded using a proprietary format owned by a company that manufactures military hardware. We've spent most of the day acquiring and installing the software required to view them."

He tapped on a massive manual for the software sitting next to his laptop. "What we do know is that the files are time coded and synchronized. This software is compiling and organizing the video files. I haven't seen this software before but it appears to be designed to play several time-synched videos simultaneously."

"If you haven't seen the videos yet, why am I here?"

The Monsignor smiled as he beckoned Father Nic to bring a chair for Jean-Paul. "Like the three of us, you are here by invitation. I know this is confusing, but I have a feeling the videos will answer some of your questions...and some of ours. This is why we brought you here so late in the day; we haven't been able to watch them until now."

His countenance dropped to a more stern expression as he turned his head slightly towards Father Julien. "It is 'now', yes? Are we ready?"

Father Julien replied with uncertainty in his voice as he dimmed the lights. "I think so. I've never used this software before so please bear with me."

As Jean-Paul, Father Nic, and the Monsignor took their seats the projector screen lit up with the feed from Father Julien's laptop. A message box on the centre of the screen read "Decoding and synchronization complete". He clicked the "Ok" button and a new window appeared. The right side was a vertical list of file names and dates. The left side looked a bit like a video player with playback controls, but the viewport was divided into four boxes with white borders. Each quadrant contained paused frames of different videos. Only the bottom-right corner was different; pitch black with white text reading "no source". He moved the cursor over to the play button and clicked it.

It took everyone in the room awhile to adjust to the three different feeds playing simultaneously. Each feed showed a daytime scene outdoors with many trees in the background. The top-left feed showed a man wearing a camouflage jacket overtop his clothes with a large hunting knife across the chest. He had on sunglasses and a helmet with a small camera attached to it. On his back was a very large backpack. The top-right feed showed the same man from a slightly different angle. The third feed in the bottom-left showed two women, one Caucasian, one Filipino, similarly attired, each sporting large backpacks of their own. The sound of wind, birds, and buzzing insects filled the lab.

"Ok...looks like both of you are recording. Is my light on?" the male said.

One woman nodded while the other said "affirmative".

"Wait...pause!" Jean-Paul exclaimed. "Is there any way to make this bigger?"

"Um, hold on," Father Julien said. He moved the mouse over to a small icon next to the right of the play button and clicked it. The video feeds went full screen and Jean-Paul's eyes widened in surprise.

"That's Sara!" he said, pointing at the woman on the left in the video frame.

"What?! *Madonna!*" the Monsignor gasped under his breath.

"I think the man is Darren Reichert," Father Nic said. Tapping on his tablet he brought up the group photo from Jake's phone that was taken in his house the day he vanished. "Look, he has the same face shape. So the other woman must be Darren's wife..."

"Uh...Trish!" Jean-Paul said.

"Play!...Resume!" the Monsignor impatiently commanded Father Julien, waving his hand in a circular motion at the younger priest while not taking his eyes off the screen.

Father Julien pressed the play button again and the three videos resumed.

"All right, then. It should be a few hundred metres ahead," Darren said as he turned and started walking forward. The other two feeds tracked him from behind as the view changed from brush and trees into a clearing revealing the otherworldly karst landscape that everyone in the room immediately recognized.

"Why are they at the cave reserve?" Jean-Paul asked aloud.

Suddenly the sound of dogs barking and distant voices emanated from the speakers in the lab. "What's that?" Sara's voice exclaimed.

"Shit. There must be people here. Maybe RCMP or some of the Cree volunteers from the search parties. We're going to have to be quick. Watch your footing!"

Darren then took off running across the rocky landscape. The women followed, their feeds bouncing wildly as they ran along the uneven ground. Occasionally each woman would show up in the other's feed as they turned their heads to check on each other.

The Monsignor put his hand on his stomach and looked at the floor. "Tell me when they've stopped," he groaned.

Darren reached the centre of the clearing and stopped, getting his bearings. "This is it," he said as the women caught up to him.

Sara looked over to a familiar vista and her outstretched arm appeared in the frame pointing to a spot in the distance. "Wait...Darren...isn't that where you were filming when it happened?"

The other two feeds spun and settled on the same vista, but from slightly different angles. "Yeah...that's it!"

"That means Jake disappeared—" Trish said slowly as they all turned 180 degrees, settling on the rock that Jake had been sitting on, "—there!"

Another dog barked, this time louder.

"We'd better hurry!" Sara exclaimed. They ran up to the rock and climbed atop, pausing when they reached the small summit.

"Okay...what now?" Trish asked.

"I don't know...Jake was here and then he wasn't," Darren replied.

"Maybe we should do what he did," Sara suggested hurriedly. "Let's all sit down."

The video feeds jostled as they sat down in a triangle, facing each other. More dogs could be heard barking, louder than before.

"Okay, we're sitting. What's next?" Trish asked.

"I don't know," Darren said, shrugging. "What did Jake do? What would he have done?"

"In the video," Sara began, closing her eyes tightly to try and focus her memory. "He was sitting there...he talked about taking it all in—" Suddenly her eyes opened wide. "He was probably meditating!"

"What?" Trish said with a tone of disbelief.

"Yeah! Jake likes to meditate when he can. Everyone close your eyes, and try to clear your mind of thoughts."

Each feed showed the trio closing their eyes. Along with the barking growing louder the sound of another human voice in the distance could be heard. In Sara's feed Trish was seen opening her eyes a few times, peeking at the others.

Time seemed to tick by slowly as the group sat there and slowed their breathing. Suddenly the audio feed went dead silent. The birds, insects, and wind had stopped. The dogs changed from barking to yelping and whimpering.

"Do you feel that?" Sara asked the group, her voice amplified by the relative quiet.

The others opened their eyes and looked around. "It's like a tingling—" Darren started to say.

A loud yelp from off to one side made the trio turn their heads. A few hundred metres away at the edge of the clearing a man in an orange vest appeared, being pulled on a leash led by a large German shepherd. "Hey!" he called out as he saw the group.

Before anyone could respond each feed glitched with static and suddenly a loud whooshing sound filled the lab, causing everyone watching to cover their ears. The static subsided into blackness, then each feed switched to a dark green colour. The pictures were out of focus as blurred objects thrashed chaotically about. As the cameras struggled to find a focus there were a few brief moments of clarity revealing that the bodies of the three people were under water, swimming upwards, surrounded by streams of bubbles.

Based on his feed, Darren was the first to break the surface. Coughing and sputtering he started treading water. The camera, automatically having adjusted to night vision mode while he was underwater, showed an eerie green waterscape of ripples and twinkling dots in the night sky that became distorted as drops of water rolled down the front of his lens.

"Trish! Sara!" he called out. A few seconds later the other two feeds broke the surface and additional coughing and choking could be heard along with splashing as the women struggled to get into a treading rhythm with the awkward backpacks on.

"The fuck!" Trish cried out. "Darren?!"

"I'm here babe!" Darren called out in reply. "Sara...you good?"

After coughing a bit more, Sara responded. "Yeah...yes, I'm here!"

"Where the hell are we?! How are we setting stars?!" Trish called out.

"This must be where Jake came up!" Darren yelled. "My eyes are still adjusting. Can anyone see land?"

As the trio looked back and forth the night vision mode revealed a treed island a short distance away, but their frantic movements indicated that the human operators could not see it yet.

"Oh...my...God," Jean-Paul said as he realized what he had just witnessed. All three priests made the sign of the cross.

Sara's feed was the first to lock onto the island and her hand appeared in the frame, pointing to it. "There!" she cried as she started swimming towards it.

The other two soon followed and for several minutes the three images were an unwatchable chaos of frothing water and moving limbs as all three did the breast stroke to the shore. Once again the Monsignor had to look away from the screen.

Trish was first to reach the shallows and was able to lift her upper body out of the water. "God damn that's cold!" she cursed. She turned to scan the water for Darren and Sara, walking back into the depths to grab Sara's hand and help pull her closer to shore. Sara crawled through the shallows, eventually collapsing on the rocky beach and rolling onto her back. Hundreds of stars sparkled like glitter in the sky above her as she panted.

Trish and Darren's feeds showed them removing their backpacks and their clothing swiftly, and in tandem. Underneath their clothes were dark garments that hugged their skin. "Give her a hand, eh?" Darren said to Trish.

Trish left her clothes and backpack by Darren and walked over to Sara who was still lying on the beach. The watchers simultaneously saw Trish appear in Sara's feed, towering over her and blocking out the stars. "C'mon. Let's get you out of those clothes before you get hypothermia," she said, holding an outstretched hand.

Darren in the meantime had produced a flashlight and was investigating the area. "You guys! Get over here!" he called.

Trish and Sara moved gingerly along the rocks as Darren used his flashlight to illuminate their path until they reached his position. He turned the beam of this flashlight to the remains of a campfire. "You were right, Sara," Darren said. "This is Jake's first campsite."

"Holy shit," Trish said quietly.

Darren dug into his backpack and pulled out a small device. He began turning a crank on it and after a few seconds pressed a button revealing it to be a second flashlight. He handed it to Trish.

"Jake left enough kindling here for me to start a fire," he said. "You two get some larger pieces of wood...but don't wander far."

"Sara needs to get out of her clothes first," Trish said. "She's already shivering."

"Okay," Darren agreed, producing a lighter from his backpack and turning back to the fire pit. "We should shut our cameras off for now and conserve power until we're settled."

"Roger," Trish replied with the tone of a soldier.

Darren and Trish's feed ended and each square was replaced by a black screen with white text reading "no source". In Sara's feed she turned and faced Trish who reached a hand up to Sara's camera, ending her feed as well.

"That's the first set of files," Father Julien said slowly as he studied the software on his laptop. "Let's see if I can start the next set." Pressing the "next" button brought up only one feed in the top-right box. He set the interface to full screen again and pressed the play button. Since there was only one feed it filled the entire screen.

The camera was still in night vision mode and the scene was initially washed out by the green-white light produced by a roaring campfire. As the camera panned up and focussed, it revealed Trish and Sara sitting on a log on the opposite site of the fire. Sara had removed her clothes and was in the same black bodysuit that Darren and Trish wore. Each woman had a towel wrapped around their shoulders and was holding a cup with visible steam emanating from within.

"My recording light on?" Darren's voice asked from off-camera.

Both women looked up at him and nodded. "Okay then," Darren continued. "Sara, you're on."

Sara took a sip from her cup before speaking. "My name is Sara Taylor," she began as she pointed to her right. "This is my best friend Trish Reichert, and her husband Darren is recording this video. We're all from Winnipeg, Manitoba, Canada. Today is June 4th, 2019, and if you're seeing this then we've successfully traveled back in time about ten thousand years in order to find and save my husband Jake. He went missing three weeks ago and was trapped here. I'm hoping that Monsignor Wowchuk, Father Nic, Father Julien, and Jean-Paul Ducharme are watching this."

"I don't believe this," Jean-Paul said, shocked. The priests all wore similar expressions on their faces.

"As you know, Jake left behind a message to be opened ten days after he originally disappeared," she continued. "He was attacked by dire wolves and seemed to be suffering from an infection in his last video, and we presumed he had died. But...he had recorded almost six weeks' worth of video and images. When I got back to Winnipeg last week I played all the videos for Darren and Trish. That's when Trish had her brilliant thought. Trish, do you want to explain it?"

Darren turned his head to point the camera at Trish, who looked from Sara to the camera. "Well...I basically wondered if one day for Jake was one day for us. According to the date on Jake's phone, he was attacked by the dire wolves sometime around June 9th, and his last recording was on June 16th, but it's only June 4th today. If one day for Jake has been one day for us then the attack hasn't happened to him yet"

"Right," Sara resumed. "And that got us thinking...if we could figure out how Jake got to the past we could follow him here and save him. And well...we're here. We have twelve days to get find him before he's attacked!"

Darren's voice interrupted from off-screen. "Unfortunately, just like with Jake this was a one-way trip. We won't be able to return to 2019. But Jake's my best friend and though the odds are against him, I can't leave him out here alone. Besides, Trish and I have our training and have survived in the wilderness before; we'll do fine without civilization and we can keep Sara safe."

Sara smiled at the camera. "We're intending to make recordings just like Jake did, and no matter what we find we're going to bury them with Jake's phone at Stony Mountain. Thanks to Darren and Trish's contacts in the military we were able to get these:" She tapped the helmet on the side of her head. "High definition helmet-mounted cameras that are recording with synchronized clocks. The files are encrypted and need special software to play but I'm sure Father Julien will figure that out."

Father Julien chuckled. Jean-Paul smiled.

Trish adjusted her position on the log. "I think the fact that we were at the cave reserves around the same time of day that Jake and Darren originally were, and we arrived here at night just like Jake did is a good sign. Our watches still say that it's 1330 CST right now even though it's clearly after midnight here. It might mean that whatever connects our two times is in sync."

"Or," Darren said, "it might just be a coincidence and we're too late."

On that statement Sara slumped her shoulders forward in sadness. Trish shot Darren an angry look, her narrowed eyes glowing supernaturally in the night vision feed. "What?" Darren exclaimed in protest. "I'm just trying to manage expectations here."

"Look, why don't you turn off the camera and get the tent set up. We can try this again in the morning."

"Fine," Darren said, ending the recording.

The next set of videos started with Trish's feed and showed a daylight scene. The first frame was frozen on her view of Darren and Sara, both of whom were looking at her with their hands at the sides of their head. Father Julien hit the play button and the scene sprang to life. Almost immediately afterwards Darren and Sara's feeds started playing.

"Okay, I think we're good," Trish began.

"You do the honours, Sara," Darren said, gesturing towards the campsite as he turned to let her pass.

Sara walked up and past Darren as he kept her in frame. She spoke loudly and excitedly. "This is the campfire that Jake created on the island when he first arrived here. We used it last night to dry out our clothes and warm up. We weren't as affected by the shock from the cold water as Jake was because we knew what to expect and we were all wearing wetsuits underneath."

"That's what those black suits were," the Monsignor said out loud.

Sara stood as still as possible and slowly panned her head across the beach and water stretching out to the horizon. "This is the same spot Jake first recorded. There's land north of here, but it's very distant. Darren has one of those collapsible pirate telescope things with him. He climbed a tree here and said that he can see white along the horizon far to the north."

"It might be the retreating glacier, or just snow that hasn't melted yet," he interjected.

Sara turned back to Darren. "But the really cool thing is this—" Tilting her head down at the ground, she focused on a series of light coloured stones that had been arranged to form an arrow pointing south.

She then stepped off the rocks and onto the grassy embankment of the island. She walked briskly, picking up speed as she traveled. Darren and Trish followed, their video feeds bouncing with their movement. About a minute later all three were on the south side of the island. Across the water was land, so close that trees were distinguishable in the video feeds.

"And look," Sara said pointing down to the ground. There on each feed was a second arrow of stones pointing to the land across the water. "These are the markers Jake left when he thought there were people looking for him."

"Guess he thought right," Trish smirked.

Darren looked down at the ground and kicked at a small stone at his feet. "I know you guys mean well and you have a lot of hope right now, but we have to remember that we're taking a big gamble hoping to find Jake alive. We don't really know if one day here is one day in 2019. For all we know weeks, months, or years have passed in this time since Jake's last video. We might have sentenced ourselves to Jake's fate just to bury his skeleton."

Trish shot Darren another angry glance as she walked over to Sara and put an arm around her. "That firepit is not months old, and it's clearly late spring here just like in Jake's videos. He's out there, Sara, and he's alive. I know he is."

"Look!" Darren suddenly exclaimed, pointing out over the water. The women turned to look in the same direction. Over the trees across the water was a giant dark cloud rising up. As the cameras focused in they revealed thousands of small black dots rising up into the sky.

"The passenger pigeons!" Sara exclaimed.

Trish smiled at Sara as she grabbed her hand and squeezed it. "Just like in Jake's video. I know this is the right time. Jake's out there."

"Damn. I will say, the odds are looking better. Okay…how about we change the subject? So for anyone who's watching, you're probably wondering how you think these two ladies and I are going to catch up to Jake. Assuming our two times have been in sync, he's had weeks of travel ahead of us."

"That's where we have an advantage," Trish said, picking up where Darren left off. "Until Jake realized that no one was coming for him, he spent almost a week on this island before heading south."

"And he spent a few days with the woolly mammoths."

"Mastodons!" the women said in unison.

"Mastodons…whatever."

Sara turned away from the massive flock across the lake and looked back at Darren. "Well we're not going to wait around in any one place that long. Plus we're better prepared. We have more food, emergency rations, first aid, survival guides, tools, more solar chargers…"

"…hand-crank USB chargers too," Trish pointed out.

"…and weapons," Darren concluded, with an over-the-top machismo tone to his voice. "I've got a rifle, Trish has a handgun, and we both have high-powered modern hunting bows with a dozen carbon arrows each for when the ammunition runs out."

Trish grabbed the backpack that Sara was wearing and spun her around to show it off for Darren's camera. "These backpacks are watertight and can be used for floatation. We'll put all our clothes into them, minus the wetsuits of course, and use them as floatation devices to help make it across the water."

"Just like Jake did with the log," Jean-Paul said under his breath.

"Just like Jake did with the log," Darren said immediately after.

Trish lifted her shirt to expose the skintight black fabric underneath. "These wetsuits should reduce the loss of body heat and allow us to make better time when swimming. Plus we'll dry off and warm up faster on the other side."

Darren looked down at his wrist as he set a timer on his wristwatch. "Okay, let's shut the cameras down and get ready. We cross in an hour."

Trish walked up and grabbed Darren's face, leaning in and kissing him, their video feeds getting blurry from their proximity to each other. Sara's feed turned away from the couple and looked back across the water to the pigeon flock.

Trish pulled away from the embrace. "See you on the other side, babe." She reached up, and turned off Darren's camera. A few seconds later both Trish and Sara's feeds ended.

"Any wagers on if they make it?" Father Nic asked as Father Julien fiddled with the software to load up the next set of videos.

"Not on your life," Jean-Paul said, eyes still fixed on the screen. The Monsignor chuckled and nodded in agreement.

Only one camera feed was available in the next set. As it sprang to life and filled the projector screen it was once again an image of the water with land in the distance. The water was calm, with gentle waves lapping at the rocky shoreline. A large fish jumped in the distance causing a small splash.

"See that?" Darren's voice filled the lab as he pointed to the land across the water. "That's where we were a few hours ago."

He panned the camera over to Sara who was sitting by a campfire. A small tent had been erected and Trish was attaching a rain flap to the top. She noticed Darren filming her.

"It's so beautiful here."

"It sure is, babe. Jake really knows how to pick a good camping spot. For those watching in the future, once again we're using his fire pit."

"Tent's ready," Trish announced.

Sara picked up a small book that was sitting on her lap. "According to the survival guide there are a few mushrooms in the brush here that are edible." She then picked up a small plastic container off the ground filled with mushrooms and blueberries she had harvested. "I saw raspberry plants, but there's no berries yet."

"Probably too early in the year," Darren said. He panned back to look over the lake for a few moments before breaking the silence. "All right. Let's eat and turn in early. We've got a long hike ahead of us."

Trish walked up and put a hand on his shoulder. "Babe, we're on the mainland now. We may encounter larger predators, like the dire wolves."

"Right. I'll get the rifle assembled. At sundown I'll take first watch." At that the feed ended.

Father Julien advanced to the next set of files and pressed play. Again it was a single feed from Darren's camera overlooking the lake, but the green tint to everything gave away the fact that the camera was in night vision mode. Aside from crickets and the lapping of the water on the shore it was very quiet. As everyone watched the lake another fish was seen jumping, its splash audible almost a second after the fish hit the water due to its distance from the camera. Darren slowly panned upwards to look at the sky. The night vision picked up more stars than were normally visible with the naked eye, rendering any attempt to pick out familiar constellations by the men in the room fruitless.

"So many stars," he said in a hushed tone. "No airplanes. No satellites." At that moment a meteorite streaked across the sky, followed by a glittery tail that seemed to persist for a second or so after it had burned out. "Did you see that? Wow!"

After staring at the sky a bit more he lowered his head to once again look over. "Trish and Sara are asleep. I figured I'd just take a moment to talk to you all back in 2019. I know we've never met, and you don't know me from Adam—"

He paused for a moment and chuckled to himself. "Adam? Hell...I don't even think Adam's been born yet. Anyhow, I wanted you to know why we decided to come back here. Here...away from family, friends, the luxury and tech of the twenty-first century—"

The sound of him sipping at a drink could be heard over the speakers. "Well, I'm mostly doing this for Jake. I know it wasn't my fault but I feel guilty that he was stranded here all alone. And Trish, she wouldn't let me come here without her, and she's doing this for

Sara. Sara wouldn't survive out here even though she's really focused on saving Jake. Though if I can be real for a moment, Jake's probably already dead.

"And as for home? Well given the shit I've seen the world's probably a decade or two from collapse and chaos. The writing's on the wall, man."

He took another sip, swallowed loudly, and sighed, lowering his voice. "Everybody dies eventually. So why not die trying to help a friend? And even if we don't save him, Jake was right. Being here is a gift. This is the most beautiful place I've ever seen. Somehow...I feel more human here."

The sound of something moving through the brush caused Darren to turn away from shore and look back towards the forest. Shining a flashlight at the trees, the bright eyes of a large buck emerging from the brush reflected back at him, glowing creepily in the night vision of the camera. Darren very carefully raised the rifle to his shoulder and sighted the animal. Both him and the deer remained motionless for over a minute before Darren exhaled and lowered the weapon. The deer bent down to graze at some grass, then walked back into the forest.

"Jake first," he said resolutely as he turned off the feed.

The next video was another single feed, this time from Sara's camera. It started off with her looking at the ground, but the brightness and full colour indicated that it was now daytime. As playback started the sounds of insects buzzing and birdsong filled the room, similar to Jake's videos. Another arrow of rocks pointed to an animal trail disappearing into the woods. "There's Jake's next marker. Darren and Trish are just packing up the camp and then we're heading out again."

She looked up at the trees where the passenger pigeons lit and darted away in a complicated and frenetic dance. "I've gotten a few shots of them, and I wish I could take the time to photograph these birds better for you guys in 2019. But I know Jake's out there and there's literally nobody else on Earth right now who can help him. We have to keep moving."

She ended the recording.

The next video was again from Sara's feed. When Father Julien started playback, Trish and Darren's feeds started up a few seconds after hers. The three scenes revealed Trish and Sara sitting around a campfire, with Darren standing in front of them. The sun, visible in Darren's feed and low in the western sky, gave a golden sheen to the trees around them in the small clearing they were located in.

"Everybody recording for this momentous occasion?" Darren asked.

The women each gave a thumb's up to confirm. "Okay, great," he said, sitting down near Trish as she handed him a plate. On the plate were some mushrooms, blueberries, what looked like a small salad, and a small portion of meat.

"So today, a flock of those passenger pigeons were flying really low and really close together, and I was able to stun one with the butt of my rifle as they passed overhead. Sara and Trish cleaned and cooked the bird, and we're going to be the first people in like a hundred years or more to eat one."

"It's amazing how easy that was to get one," Sara said.

Trish elbowed Sara playfully. "It's probably why they went extinct."

Darren lifted up a fork and knife. "Well ladies...dig in!"

The next several seconds had no speaking as each person cut into the small portion of meat on their plate and started chewing.

Darren was the first to speak. "You know, it's not too bad. Tastes a bit like chicken...but gamier. Maybe pheasant."

"Do you think it's safe to eat this?" Trish asked.

"We cooked it thoroughly," Sara responded. "There shouldn't be any parasites or bacteria alive to infect us."

"That's not what I meant...what if this is like a 'butterfly effect' thing where we make a tiny change in the past but it affects the future? Like what if—"

She glanced around and lowered her voice. "What if Hilary Clinton didn't win the 2016 election because we ate this bird?"

"What?!" Jean-Paul exclaimed loudly, his eyes widening.

Trish stared intently at Darren's camera for a moment before bursting out laughing. "Oh man...oh I'm sorry...I couldn't help myself."

Sara and Darren laughed along with her. "Sorry future guys," she said between chuckles. "That's just a little time travel humour. We know that asshole Trump won the election."

"Another reason I don't miss 2019," Darren snickered.

"*Tabernac*!" Jean-Paul exclaimed in frustration at having been fooled by the ruse, shaking his head. He suddenly remembered where he was and his face went a little red. "Sorry," he sheepishly said to the priests. His cursing and apology didn't seem to be noticed by the priests.

Sara covered her mouth with her hand while she spoke. "Well given that we no longer have access to a twenty-first century diet, variety here will be important to keep us healthy. So thank you Darren for the meat."

"That's what she said," Darren joked. Both women rolled their eyes.

"Real mature, ass," Trish shot back at him. Taking a bite of the greens on her plate she turned to Sara. "And a thank you to Sara for the salad."

"It was easier than you'd think. The survival guides we put together included a list of edible wild plants native to Manitoba. I had no idea how many could just be eaten raw. We've been getting salad from bags in the grocery store for the last several years when half the stuff growing in our backyard could have been eaten."

Darren finished scraping the last of his food off his plate and onto his fork. "I gotta say, when we decided to do this thing I figured we'd be scrounging in the dirt just trying to stay alive but it seems like food is plentiful here and it isn't even summer yet. You don't have to look far to find something to eat."

"We don't know if it'll be that way forever," Trish cautioned. "And it certainly won't be this good in the winter, so we should always try to eat as much as we can to keep our fat stores up."

Darren stood up. "Well, I guess eating this pigeon didn't kill us instantly, so we can probably stop recording now. Let's get ready to turn in. I'll take first watch again." His feed stopped followed shortly afterwards by the women's feeds.

When Father Julien advanced to the next series, Darren's feed sprung up again, this time in night vision mode. He was looking over the dying campfire and the tent not far away, clearly keeping watch as Sara and Trish slept.

"So tomorrow is day three of the mission. We've got a lot of ground to cover and I'm still worried about whether or not we'll find Jake alive...but I can't get over just how quiet and beautiful it is out here. Listen."

The sounds of night time insects, bat calls, and the occasional owl hoot filled the lab.

"The funny thing is that you can hear all of this in 2019. If it wasn't for the fact that I know we travelled back in time I wouldn't think I was anywhere else. It's not like there's dinosaurs roaring or anything like that. Anyhow, it's almost time for Trish to start second watch so I'll stop recording. Talk to you later, future people!"

He looked up at the stars for a moment before ending the recording.

The next series started with Trish's feed. It was daytime again and the video's first frame had the viewers in the lab looking at an animal trail winding through a forest of poplars and birch. As playback started it cut into Trish already talking in a hushed tone. "...urn your cameras on, guys."

The screen split in two as Darren's feed came on, then split again a moment later as Sara's started. Sara was standing behind Trish, and Darren was a few metres behind Sara. Trish's left arm was raised with a clenched fist signalling the group to stop.

"What is it?" Darren whispered.

"Listen!" The sounds of birds and insects filled the lab as the humans stopped moving. Suddenly the cracking and snapping of branches in the distance caused each person to hold perfectly still. Sara tilted her head to try and hear where the noise was coming from.

Darren raised the rifle as he slowly moved up past Trish and the two women started following him at the same careful pace. From

Sara's feed the men in the lab could see Trish unholster her pistol and hold it pointed at the ground. In addition to cracking and snapping noises, grunting could be heard.

"Whatever's over there is big," Darren whispered loudly. Sara moved closer to Trish and put a hand on her shoulder.

Suddenly the blast of an elephant trumpeting filled the air. Everyone jumped, including the men in the lab who were watching the playback.

Trish looked back at Sara, whose face turned from shock to joy. "The mastodons!" she cried.

Darren walked up ahead faster, keeping the rifle ready. The women quickened their pace to keep up. As he reached the end of the animal trail the scene changed to a bright gray sky, filled with cloud cover. The forest gave way to waist-high prairie grass, and opened up to a wide plain. A few hundred metres away from the treeline were a group of mastodon.

Darren suddenly jarred to a stop and sharply turned his head left. Right beside him at the forest's edge was a mastodon that towered over him by almost a metre. It was using its trunk to pull leaves off of the branches of an elm. As his camera focused on its face, the eye of the great beast moved and looked squarely at Darren. Darren's sudden stop caused Trish and Sara to bump into him.

"Oh shit!" he exclaimed under his breath. The women gasped. The mastodon grunted at them.

Very slowly, Darren turned his body to face the beast, and he grabbed Trish and pulled her behind him. She in turn grabbed Sara and the two moved further along the tree line, away from Darren and the beast. Once they had gotten about twenty metres away, Darren slowly backed up and joined the women. The mastodon grunted one more time and returned its attention to the tree from which it was feeding.

"Are you okay, babe?" Trish asked, placing a hand on Darren's shoulder as he reached the women.

Darren slowly turned and looked at the them, his face pale. He nodded. All three looked out upon the expanse and all the animals before them. In addition to groups of mastodon there were herds of deer, massive flocks of birds, and even a large moose with strange antlers standing in a swampy area in the distance.

Realizing they were safe, the trio laughed, cried, cheered, and hugged as they celebrated finding the herd. Several of the beasts turned their heads to eye the noisy humans suspiciously. "The mastodons are here! Just like in Jake's video!"

The women looked at Darren, who was wiping a tear from his eye. "My god...they're real. And they're incredible!" he said, choked up.

Sara grabbed Darren's and Trish's hands. "This means we're closer to Jake! Look, I know how amazing this is...and I want to just stay and watch these beautiful creatures...but we should keep going!"

She started walking away from them but Darren raised his hand. "Hold up!" He took only a moment to glance at Sara before turning back to look at the mastodons. "We've pushed really hard today and it's already mid-afternoon. We should find Jake's campsite and set up there. Jake normally only set up camp after a day of walking, so if we leave now we won't find his next site before dark."

Trish put her hand on Sara's shoulder. "He's right. We're no good to Jake if we get lost or collapse from exhaustion. We're still making good time. Mastodons were probably migratory, like elephants. The fact that they're still in this area means Jake was here not that long ago. Let's find Jake's site."

Sara acquiesced, and they fanned out along the treeline, taking care to avoid the feeding mastodon, but couldn't spot any obvious signs of human presence. It wasn't until Darren started walking towards a small group of mastodons in the open that he saw a simple lean-to in the open prairie.

"Here!" he called out. The women ran up to join him and arrived at the basic shelter, which consisted of little more than sticks holding up pine branches beside a small fire pit.

Trish sat down under the lean-to. "It's so close to the mastodons. He's lucky they didn't step on him while he was sleeping."

"Actually, it was really smart," Darren said. "These hairy elephants weren't going to come near Jake or the fire, and his distance from the trees probably ensured that whatever predators are in the forest wouldn't come out to bother him and risk an encounter with the big guys."

"If the mastodons were used to Jake being here, then hopefully they won't mind us. This is probably the best place for us to stay."

Sara put her hands on her hips. "Well that's settled then. I'll go to the forest and forage."

Darren handed Trish the rifle. "You go with her and I'll set up the tent and dig a latrine. Remember, there might be wolves."

"Affirmative. I'll watch her six. All right we should save power. Cameras off." After her feed ended, Sara's ended shortly after. Darren took a few more moments of staring at the herd before he too reached up and stopped his recording.

The next video, from Trish's feed, showed that the sun had moved into the western sky above the prairie, indicating that it was late afternoon. The scene was the same, but the positions of the animals had changed between recordings. The deer had moved further west into the distance and the moose was gone. The mastodon groups had changed places slightly, but their numbers still appeared to be the same. As playback resumed Darren's voice could be heard in the distance.

"Did you start recording?"

Darren's camera then turned on, showing that he was looking at Trish who was about thirty metres away and over by the campsite.

"Yeah, yeah," Trish responded with an annoyed tone as her feed panned over to look at him. He was very close to one of the mastodons. "Why am I recording you?"

"For this! I bet you I can touch one!"

"Are you fucking crazy?!" Trish yelled at him. She glanced over to see Sara walking up from the direction of the treeline.

"What's going on? What's Darren doing?"

"That idiot wants to pet one of those things," Trish said angrily as she turned the camera back to Darren.

"What?! Don't do it!"

Ignoring them, Darren slowly walked up to the closest mastodon, his hands raised. When he got to within a few feet of the beast it grunted at him and he backed off a bit, startled.

"Oh shit, oh shit, oh shit!" Sara's voice could be heard whispering from beside Trish.

"Don't do it!" Father Nic yelled to the screen as he shook his head. The other three men's mouths were agape.

Darren resumed his approach, a little slower, making sure the great beast could see him at all times. The deep breathing of the mastodon could be heard rumbling through the speakers in the lab. As he got closer individual hairs were visible on the screen, as were the characteristic wrinkles of its trunk.

"That's it...easy, buddy—" Darren said slowly and softly as he reached out to the mastodon. Everyone watching in the lab held their breath as his hand slowly pushed against the creature's hair and came to rest where the trunk met the head.

"Holy shit," Jean-Paul said.

"Holy shit, he did it," Trish whispered at the same time as Jean-Paul.

Darren started slowly petting the trunk of the massive animal. "Wow". The creature blinked and its long eyelashes brushed against his arm.

He turned and looked back at the women. Trish had a dumbfounded look on her face and Sara was holding on to her arm, looking equally shocked. "You guys need to try this!" he yelled back at them.

His sudden outburst startled the mastodon and it cried out, knocking Darren onto the ground with its trunk and raising up on its hind legs. Darren's feed became blurred as he fell and tumbled but he quickly turned back to see the mastodon rising up above him. He rolled back towards the campsite and started getting up to his feet to run. The beast's front legs fell to the ground and created such an impact that the thud reverberated through the lab. The vibration caused Darren to stumble slightly but he regained his footing and sprinted back to the women within a few seconds. The mastodon did not pursue.

"Are you fucking crazy?!" Trish yelled at him as he arrived. "Are you hurt?"

"I'm good, I'm good," he panted, a huge smile across his face. "Oh man, that was great. That was like petting a fucking Snuffleupagus!"

"Ugh," Trish said in disgust as she turned away from him. She reached up and ended her feed as she walked back to the campfire.

"What?!" he said in protest to her reaction. He looked over at Sara. Her eyes were wide in shock but her expression was angry.

"Can you not fucking die before we find Jake, please?"

"Oh come on, I was fine," he called out as he reached up and stopped the feed.

"I can't believe he did that!" Jean-Paul said as the video ended.

"Big balls on that guy," the Monsignor said in agreement. Everyone turned and stared at him wide-eyed.

He grumbled at them. "What? Play the next one!"

Once again only a single feed was available, this time in Trish's square in the viewport. Father Julien played it and they were greeted by a night vision feed, looking down at the ground. The camera tilted up, revealing the prairie stretching ahead. The crackling of the dying campfire could be heard to the left, the only sound that overpowered the chirping of crickets and the calls of frogs and toads in nearby marshier areas. In the grass were the mastodons, huddled together in small groups across the plain. "I'm guessing those are family units," Trish started quietly. "That one there is lying down. Sleeping, I guess. I've only seen the big ones lie down for maybe forty, fifty minutes. They take turns while the others keep watch. I haven't seen the little ones since the sun went down so they're probably sleeping on the ground close to their mommies.

"You know, none of this seemed real until these mastodons. Aside from the insane number of birds, it just felt like a hunting trip up in northern Manitoba. It felt like we were just on vacation and in a few days we'd be back in Winnipeg. Back working our day jobs. But now—"

She paused as one of the giant beasts grunted and growled loudly, giving it time to quiet down. "—now it's real. Extra real since that moron tried to get himself killed by one, too.

"Sara and Darren are asleep in the tent while I keep watch. I figure it's sometime around 0200 hours. It's been quiet and you won't believe how many times I've reached for my phone so I could browse Pinterest or Facebook or Instagram. Heh. Old habits. Never going to see any social media again...but you know I don't think I really care all that much."

Trish looked up, the blanket of stars in the sky above her partially obscured by the branch and leaves of a tree over her head. "Sara's been telling me I should record a message for family or friends, or at least for you priest guys who are hopefully watching this. So here it goes.

"Darren and I have known each other since high school, and before that, cadets. We were deployed together in Afghanistan after 9/11. In '07 we were down in Panjwayi when an IED took out the lead vehicle in our convoy. In the chaos I saw that son of a bitch run into that mass of burning, twisted metal, and pull one of our guys out...a guy Darren was pretty good friends with. I was our unit's field medic so I followed Darren and I kept him alive until evac picked us up. Funny...right now I can't remember that guy's name...we never talk about it. I guess the point of my story is that it was at that moment I realized Darren was the man I wanted to spend the rest of my life with. And now, just as then, he's running headfirst into danger to save his friend, and I'm following him."

She paused for a while, scanning the horizon as the mastodon herd went about its nighttime activities. "As for leaving behind family and friends...hell, Sara's my only real friend, and odds are nobody is ever going to see this recording. I guess our disappearance will just end up being a mystery to everyone back home. Just like Jake's. As for Jake, it's going to be a lot harder to track him now. After he saw the mastodons and realized he was in the past, he probably stopped leaving arrows for search and rescue. I guess we'll just head due south until we find Stony Mountain."

Trish yawned quietly and then looked at her watch. "It's time to get some shut-eye. I'm going to get Darren up to take second watch. Talk to you later...whoever's watching." Her hand came up to the side of her head. "Probably nobody," she mumbled as her feed ended.

The next feed was Darren's, though the bright colours of the scene indicated it was now daytime. The video came to life and after a bit of jostling Sara and Trish were seen walking ahead of him along a narrow path through a dense forest. In the canopy above were constant shadows darting through the trees. He narrated as he followed the women. "We've left the mammoths and we're walking along a deer trail. I determined that it was the route Jake followed, because it leads south and I am a master tracker."

Trish turned to face Darren with a sarcastic look on her face. "...and because Sara found a couple of Jake's boot prints near the entrance. And it's mastodons." She grinned at the camera, then stuck her tongue out.

"Mastodons...whatever."

Sara looked up above them. "There are so many passenger pigeons. Hard to believe they're extinct."

"They aren't extinct now," Darren said, correcting her. "They'll be around for another ten thousand years, give or take."

Trish took a deep breath. "I just love how it smells here. The air is always fresh and clean."

"It wasn't that fresh by the mammoths!"

"Mastodons!" the women said in unison.

"Whatever!"

The brush got a little thicker and Trish began pushing branches aside as she walked. "You know, it really sucks that we had to leave. I could see why Jake spent days just watching them."

"We'll see them again, once we save Jake," Sara said. At that point the feed ended.

As the next set came up the single feed was from Darren's camera again, but the initial frame showed Darren's face filling the screen, a look of horror and panic upon him. Jean-Paul and the priests straightened up in their chairs at the sight of it.

"Oh no," Jean-Paul said under his breath. Father Julien gulped loudly and pressed play.

The scene sprang to life as Darren panted heavily, moving quickly through the woods. "Oh my God! Oh my God! Holy shit! I can't believe what I just saw! I can't! I'm going to put my helmet back on to make sure I'm recording it so you can see it too!"

The scene jostled as he put the helmet back on his head, revealing thick brush ahead of him. He pushed through it muttering "Oh God!" over and over until he approached a clearing. Two dark figures were visible between the branches as he approached the edge.

"What are those?" the Monsignor asked with baited breath, squinting at the screen.

As Darren broke through the bushes, the camera focussed on Trish and Sara sitting on logs around a small campfire. Both women promptly turned to face him with puzzled expressions. Sara was taking a sip from a metal cup.

"Oh my God!" Darren cried out, pointing at the women. "It's a pair of endangered Winnipeg cougars!"

Sara's eyes went wide and she spat out everything that was in her mouth all over the fire, half choking, half laughing. The fire loudly sizzled in response to the spray.

Trish tried her best to hold back a smile. "For fuck's sake! We're surrounded by prehistoric predators and you're doing a bit?"

"What? It doesn't all have to be nature documentaries and sob-fests."

Trish raised her left hand and flipped him off, which he responded to by laughing heartily. Sara joined in the laughter also. As Darren walked up to the fire and the laughter died down, Sara finished what was left in her cup.

"Okay ladies," Darren barked like a drill sergeant. "Break time's over. You guys go use the facilities while I pack everything up. We head out in ten." Darren reached up and stopped the video.

"Well he sure had me going for a moment," Father Julien said before the next video set was up. Father Nic snorted in agreement and nodded.

"What does this mean...'cougar'?" the Monsignor asked the room.

The other priests chuckled and looked to Jean-Paul to respond. "It's an insult, Monsignor. It means...an older woman who preys on younger men."

The Monsignor laughed and slapped his knee in response.

Jean-Paul turned to the others. "For a moment there it felt like I was watching someone's lame Facebook video."

The next set consisted of only Sara's feed as she looked at Trish and Darren. Trish was standing with a large walking stick as tall as she was and Darren was holding his rifle in retention. As the playback started, the loud sound of rushing water filled the lab. Sara's voice could be heard just above the din. "Seriously! Turn your cameras on. It's important we document this!"

Darren and Trish looked at each other. Darren raised his eyebrows at Trish who tilted her head at him to signal him to comply. They both reached up and pressed the record button on their helmet cams, which caused Sara's full screen video to retreat to its quarter of the screen as the other two feeds turned on. Their feeds revealed Sara standing behind a wide running stream.

"How do you know this is it?" Trish asked.

"Yeah. You said the same thing about the last three creeks we crossed."

"No, this time I'm sure of it. This one is the creek Jake fished out of!"

Darren turned away from the women and looked further downstream. Standing in the middle of the creek about a hundred metres away was a great blue heron. He began walking along the creek towards it.

Sara took off her backpack and knelt on the ground. "Look, I'll pull out my tablet and bring up Jake's video. You'll see."

Trish looked up to see Darren walking away. "Where are you going, babe? It's just a heron. We have those back home."

In Darren's feed however, a brown object was visible in the grass ahead of him, a few feet from the edge of the creek.

"I'm not looking at the damn bird!"

He approached the object and picked it up, revealing it to be the fish trap woven of branches and prairie grass that Jake had constructed. He held it up at chest height and turned to face the women. "I'm looking at this!"

Sara stopped what she was doing, picked up her backpack and ran to catch up with Darren. Trish walked briskly behind her. As they reached Darren the viewers could also see the remains of the campfire that Jake had used to cook the fish he caught.

Darren looked over to where the heron was standing. He began walking towards the bird, splashing into the water. Despite having no apparent fear of humans, the large bird decided that Darren was getting too close for comfort and it hopped up and flapped away, the sound of its wings beating being loud enough to be heard in the lab.

Trish inspected the area around the firepit while Sara watched Darren. "What are you doing?"

Looking down, Darren found the arrangement of rocks that Jake had wedged the trap into in his videos and put the trap back into position. "When in Rome!"

He paused briefly while bent over to chuckle. "Heh...when in Rome...Rome doesn't even exist yet! Though ironically if these recordings survive that's where they'll be watched!"

Jean-Paul broke the attention of the other men. "Does anyone else find it weird that they keep talking about us and to us, even though they don't even know if we'll ever see these videos?" They all nodded at him.

As Darren finished up with the trap and walked back up on shore his face bore a pensive expression. "Huh."

"What is it, babe?"

"I wonder if Jake had seen the heron fishing there, and realized that it was a good spot for his trap? If so, that's pretty damn clever."

"Well you can ask him that when you see him," Sara said confidently.

Darren smiled briefly then looked around at their surroundings. "We covered a lot of ground today, so here's as good a place as any to set up camp. Sara, you get a fire going. I'll go dig a latrine and collect firewood. Hopefully we'll have some fish in a few hours to cook for dinner. Babe, get the tent up...but closer to the trees and away from any trails. A lot of animals will likely come to this stream to drink."

"I'm on it," Sara said, as she began gathering nearby kindling and arranging the partially burnt logs in Jake's fire pit.

Trish and Darren walked over to the treeline together. There was a larger tree with a strong limb lower to the ground and Darren pulled himself up on it to get a better vantage point. Trish started retrieving the tent from her backpack and looked up at him in the tree. "What are you looking for?"

He slowly panned from left to right across the creek. "Just looking to see which way we'll be going tomorrow,"

"See anything interesting?"

The camera stopped panning when it became obvious that several light coloured rocks had been removed from the creek and arranged into an arrow shape at another deer trail at the treeline. He hopped out of the tree. "Yup. Arrow marks the spot."

"Wait. There's an arrow? I wasn't expecting Jake to make any more after he realized he was in the past."

"Beats me. All I know is there's an arrow. Though we should stop recording now and focus on our tasks."

"Agreed." Both her and Darren's feeds ended.

Sara touched one of the logs that had been left behind by Jake. "See you soon," she said quietly before ending her own feed.

"Does anyone need to use the toilet?" Father Julien asked, as he hovered the mouse over the "next" button. "The sound of the water running in that video has made me realize that we're probably due for a break."

The Monsignor slowly rose from his chair. "I do, *scusa!*"

He looked over at Jean-Paul. "When you're as old as me you can't hold it as long as you used to", he said quietly, smiling and winking. Jean-Paul gave him a tight-lipped grin and got up to stretch his legs. Father Julien turned the house lights back on and followed after the Monsignor, down the hall at the back of the lab.

Father Nic walked out into an adjoining room and Jean-Paul found himself alone. At first he didn't know what to do but before he had a chance to casually poke around the lab Father Nic returned with a serving tray containing four bottles of water. He picked up a bottle and handed it to Jean-Paul.

"*Grazie,*" Jean-Paul said as he opened his bottle. The popping of the seal breaking as he twisted the cap echoed in the room and Jean-Paul realized just how quiet it was after watching the last few hours of loud video clips.

"*Salut,*" Father Nic said, raising his bottle to Jean-Paul. Jean-Paul returned the gesture and they both took their first sips of water in silence.

"How big is this place?"

Father Nic raised an eyebrow at the question and smiled coyly. "Big enough. Normally there are a few more people working here, but it is after hours...and the secrecy surrounding these artefacts have had us operating on a much smaller scale, staff-wise. For containment reasons, of course."

"Of course." He tried his best to sound nonchalant while discussing the secret lab housing secret artefacts under Vatican City in which he was standing. He smiled to himself at the surreal aspect of his situation.

It was Father Nic's turn to ask a question. "What do you think, *Signor*? Will they find Jacob Taylor? And if they do, will he be alive or dead?"

"I honestly have no idea. But the more I've watched the more I want to find out."

Father Nic nodded slowly while looking down at the floor pensively.

"And you, *padre*? What's your take?"

Father Nic looked at Jean-Paul and was about to speak when the Monsignor and Father Julien returned from the bathroom. Upon seeing the bottles of water, the Monsignor immediately grabbed one. "Ah, *grazie, Padre Nicolas!*" He twisted the cap off and took a large swig. Father Julien picked up his bottle and carried it back to the podium.

"Are we good to continue, gentlemen?" the Monsignor asked. Jean-Paul and Father Nic looked at each other briefly, then nodded to the Monsignor. The three returned to their seats as Father Julien lowered the house lights and advanced the playlist.

The next video was from Sara's feed and the initial frame showed Darren frozen in mid-step as he was walking into the creek near where the heron was before. The time of day had changed to the golden hour, which cast long shadows from the trees along the creek's banks and gave everything a warm hue. With the video resumed time started moving again and the sound of the flowing water once filled the lab. The golden sunlight made the water sparkle.

"Did you catch anything?" Trish called from off camera.

"I'm not even there yet!" Darren snapped back at her as he gingerly stepped making sure he had his footing. Finally he reached the place where he submerged Jake's basket. He reached down and quickly lifted it out of the water, keeping the wide end upright. Water poured out from between the branches as he turned and quickly hustled back to the bank. Once he got close to the fire he dumped the contents out and a large big-mouth bass spilled out onto the grass. It immediately started flopping.

Sara and Trish whooped and hollered in celebration.

"Thank you, Jake," Darren said, impressed. "Sara, do you know how to fillet a fish?"

"No, Jake always did it whenever we went fishing."

"Trish will show you how. I'll put the trap back in the water and get some more firewood before dusk."

As Sara watched the fish lying on the grass and gasping for air, Trish could be seen in the top corner digging in her backpack for the fillet knife she soon produced. She walked up to Sara, crouched down in front of her, and handed her the knife. "The first thing we need to do is bleed the fish."

"Uh, I don't think we need to record this," Sara said as she reached up and ended the recording.

The next video was Trish's feed. It was in night vision mode and the first frame was paused on the creek. The night vision made the water look strange. As the video started the sound of the babbling creek filled the lab again.

She spoke in a hushed voice. "Okay. I'm on second watch tonight and I was dozing off a bit but I'm wide awake now. Listen!"

She stopped talking and Jean-Paul turned his head to one side and leaned forward slightly trying to hear better. After about thirty seconds of the sounds of the creek there was a sudden loud and piercing cry. It sounded like a woman screaming, or more accurately, the sound of a witch or a zombie screaming in a horror movie. All the men watching jerked in their seats, startled by the sound.

"What the hell was that!" Jean-Paul exclaimed.

Trish snorted. "I'll bet that scared the shit out of you. Nothing like a good jumpscare in a fucked up home movie like this."

She stopped talking. Once again all that could be heard was the sound of the flowing water and the occasional pop from the dying embers of the fire. Eventually the inhuman cry was heard again.

"What you're listening to is the call of the red fox. Sounds like a woman screaming, eh? Scary as hell but I'm actually happy to hear it. You know why? Jake started hearing the wolves howling around this point in his journey. And if foxes are calling then I assume there are no larger predators nearby. And that, ladies and gentlemen, is what we call 'a good thing'."

A second fox from somewhere off to the right replied to the first one's call with a similarly eerie screech. "Well, someone's getting laid tonight!" and with that she brought her hand up to her head and ended the recording.

The next video started with the feed from Trish's camera. Sara, seated on a log next to a campfire, filled the initial frame. Father Julien started the video.

"Okay, go," Trish said.

Sara looked directly into Trish's camera. "Today marks day five of us being here. We've been heading due south since leaving Jake's fishing creek this morning, and we've covered a lot of ground today. Sorry we didn't take any videos earlier; there wasn't anything all that interesting that happened. We also couldn't find Jake's next campsite, unfortunately. It's getting late in the day, and we came across this clearing, so we're setting up camp here."

"Tell them about the fish."

Sara smiled. "Oh. Right. Jake's trap came through for us again and we had a nice big fish waiting for us in the morning. I filleted it...with Trish's help...and we cooked it up for breakfast. There was even some left over for lunch! Darren also managed to get another passenger pigeon today which we're having for dinner. All this combined with the salads I've been making is going to help keep us properly fed while we're here."

Darren boasted from off camera. "I hit the damned thing with a rock!"

Trish turned her head to look at him. He was crouched a short distance from the fire, putting up the tent.

"My man, the mighty hunter," Trish sarcastically bragged while giggling.

Darren spoke as he continued working on the tent. "You know, I was thinking about it...and I know why we didn't find Jake's campsite today. Jake already had the wolves on his trail so he had travelled downwind through streams to throw them off the scent. We didn't have to do any of that today, so now we've taken a different path."

"Is there a chance we'll miss him?" Sara asked.

Trish walked over and sat next to Sara. "We know he that makes it to Stony Mountain and will be there in four days. As long as we keep heading south, we'll find it and Jake. In fact, because we aren't taking the detours Jake did, we might have shaved a day or two off the journey! Hell, we might beat him there!"

Darren laughed. "Man, wouldn't he be surprised!"

Trish looked at her watch. "We should turn in early. Today was a warm day but it'll cool off at night."

Sara nodded. "Yeah. I sweated quite a bit today. I don't know about you guys, but I haven't really bathed since our swim from the island, and I could use a bath."

Trish rubbed her hands over the fire. "We passed a pond about half a click from here that looked pretty clean, remember? Once it warms up a bit in the morning we'll go there and check it out."

"Works for me."

Trish then ended the feed.

The next video feed was from Darren's camera. The initial frame showed a bright blue sky, poplars, and tall prairie grass. When playback started the image bobbed up and down as it showed Darren carefully walking up towards a rocky area of limestone. Moving from grass to gravel the view changed to him looking out over a small pond in a natural limestone depression. On one of the larger rocks near the water's edge was a pile of outer clothes and a couple of towels. On a second rock, lying out in the sun, were panties and sports bras, wet and drying.

The camera then panned over to the water, where Trish and Sara were a few metres from the pond's edge, both nude. Sara's back was to the camera, and she was kneeling in the water, which came not quite up to her waist. Her neck and head were red from the past week's exposure to the sun and wind, but the rest of her skin was quite pale. Slightly more noticeably pale were her bare buttocks where a faint tan line remained from the past summer's swimsuit. She had a cloth in her hands and was dipping it in the water to wash her chest and armpits.

Trish was standing completely upright in the water, but facing the camera. She was bent over washing her legs with a cloth, though her head was turned as she was talking to Sara. Even though the angle prevented a lot of her body from being visible, it was obvious from her arms and legs that Trish was in very good shape and worked out regularly. At the distance Darren's camera was from them, their voices couldn't be heard over the birds and insects in the area.

"Damn," Darren said to himself audibly.

"Wow," Jean-Paul said quietly.

Sara turned slightly towards Trish and noticed Darren approaching, her arms immediately going up to cover her breasts as she sank deeper down into water to hide her naked backside. "Oh shit!"

Trish immediately stood up and stared at Darren, fully nude. Her brown skin had no tan lines visible. "What's the problem?!"

"No problem," Darren said, as he stopped in front of the rock where their outer clothes had been piled.

"Then why are you here? You're supposed to be waiting for us at the campsite, and *then* it's your turn to bathe."

"Well I was concerned there might be a couple of giant beavers here so I thought I'd make sure everyone was okay."

Trish looked puzzled until she realized the double entendre. "There aren't any giant bea....oh you ass! Real mature!" Darren burst out laughing in response.

"Seriously though, I figured I'd join you. Safety in numbers and all that. Plus I've already packed up the camp so we can leave from here when we're done and save some time." He bent down to untie his boots and remove them. Standing up he removed his helmet and put it down on the rock, the camera still pointing out at the women in the pond. Soon the rest of his clothes were tossed down with the women's clothes and he stepped into the picture, naked from behind.

Sara, who had been looking away the whole time, turned back briefly, saw Darren nude, and quickly turned away, her face blushing. "I did not need to see that!"

"Seriously, Darren?"

"Hey, we're married. Plus in the military we bathed in groups."

"Yeah, but never coed, and Sara isn't military, or married to you!"

Sara waved her hand for Darren to join them without turning to face him. "It's fine, it's fine. We might be the only people for a thousand miles and we're ten thousand years in the past. We're basically our own tribe now so we can't stay hung up on Victorian prudishness. Plus Darren's right...we can get going again sooner."

Darren got into the water and joined Trish. Once he knelt down and his lower extremities were submerged, Sara turned to face the couple, gingerly lowering her arm from her bare breasts. "Just don't be a perv about it, okay?"

Darren gave Sara a thumbs up and turned his back to her and splashed Trish, who cried out in surprise and splashed him back. Sara kept her back to the frolicking couple and finished up washing her body. She then exited the pond and walked up to the rock where Darren's camera was sitting, retrieved one of the towels, and quickly wrapped it around her body. She watched Darren and Trish playing, embracing, and kissing in the water as she started to towel off, then glanced over at the camera. Puzzled, she leaned towards the lens.

"What the—" She suddenly backed away, pulling the towel tighter around her body to make sure she was covered. "Darren! Was this thing recording the whole time?"

"Oh was it?" Darren called out unconvincingly surprised. "Ooops!"

"Oh, you pervert!" Trish yelled at him with an annoyed tone as she shoved him down into the water. "You did that on purpose! It's not like we can delete any files!"

"What?! I figured those priests and whoever back in the future deserved a bit of a show!"

"Geez!" Sara blushed as she reached out to the side of Darren's camera. "I'm so sorry about that, everyone."

The feed came to an end.

Jean-Paul was flustered by all the nudity "Um...okay. That must have been awkward for you guys."

Father Julien shrugged and smiled slyly. "Eh, there's far worse in the *Stufetta della Bibbiena*."

Father Nic snickered quietly at Father Julien's response.

"The what?"

The Monsignor waved his hand dismissively. "There is no time for such things! We must continue."

Father Julien's smile disappeared from his face. "*Si, Monsignor!*" He moved the cursor over the "next" button and clicked it.

The newest video feed was Sara's. It was daytime and she was walking behind Darren along another animal trail. Father Julien started playback and the scene sprang into action, with Darren walking casually ahead, the rifle slung over his shoulder. Birds, insects, and the sounds of their footfalls on the ground filled the lab.

Sara addressed the viewers as she walked. "Nothing much to report today. While we all took a bath this morning the sun charged up my and Trish's cameras and I decided to film a little bit of this walk...though I imagine it looks like most of the other walks we've already filmed."

Trish laughed from behind her. "At least they know we survived bathing and our asses are clean!"

"It's early afternoon right now, and we've decided that we'll set up camp at the next body of clean water we find. Manitoba had tons of creeks in the twenty-first century and there seems to be even more in this time, so we don't have to worry about ever dying of thirst."

Suddenly Darren stopped walking and made the hand signal for the others to follow suit. He gestured for them to move to the right side of the path, then turned back and looked at them and put his index finger to his mouth, indicating that they should be silent. Sara looked back at Trish who had quietly come up right behind her and was resting her hand on her holstered pistol.

As everyone stood still the sound of something moving through the forest could be heard ahead. As the sound grew louder they started hearing more things moving, and suddenly a female white-tailed deer appeared on the trail ahead of them. As it got near to the humans it paused, then very nervously walked past Darren, then the women. After it passed safely by, three fawns came bounding down the path after it.

Sara watched as they disappeared down the trail from where the humans had just come from. "Wow! I've never been that close to a deer before."

"All clear," Darren said, and the group resumed walking along the trail.

Sara brought her hand up to the side of her head. "I'm glad I happened to be recording this. I'll touch base with you guys when we've set up our next camp." The recording ended.

Father Julien advanced to the next series. It started with Trish's feed showing Sara sitting across from her on a small log beside a campfire. A few seconds after playback started, Sara reached up and pressed the side of her camera which started her stream and caused the screen to split in two.

Sara stood up and panned over the area. "So here we are at our next campsite."

A few feet behind Trish was the tent, then a short distance from the campfire was the edge of a small creek running past them. The camera panned across the small clearing they were in and the creek disappeared further upstream around a bend. "Once again we didn't find any trace of Jake."

Trish raised her index finger. "But it's all good. Remember, we're following a different route than Jake did."

"I know. It was just always comforting to find the places he had been to already. Now it feels like we're the only humans on Earth."

"Speaking of the only humans on Earth right now...if you're wondering why Darren isn't recording as well it's because—" Trish inhaled deeply and spoke the next part in a loud voice. "—he ran down his camera's battery filming his softcore porn movie at the pond this morning instead of charging it like we did."

Darren called from offscreen. "Hey! *Pond Sluts* could've made us a fortune if we sold it online!"

"You're such a pig, Darren! But I love you!"

"Love you too, babe!"

Sara rolled her eyes. "Anyhow, we didn't have any luck catching fish or animals for dinner today, but the forest has provided us with a lovely vegan meal of mushrooms, berries, and greens, as usual. Maybe tomorrow we'll have better luck."

"He could have shot that deer that passed us on the trail."

Darren walked into the shot and sat down next to Trish on her log and took a plate from Sara. "A: it was a young mother with fawns to care for, and B: we don't have time to dress and process a large animal. Our mission is to get to Jake."

Sara passed out metal camping forks to her companions. "All right, everyone, let's dig in!"

"I guess they don't need to watch us eat," Trish stated as she reached up and turned off her feed. Darren's camera went off next and Trish could be seen in Sara's feed starting to take a bite of her meal just before the entire recording ended.

The next video started with Sara's feed alone, and the green hue to everything revealed that her camera was in night mode, the initial frame looking over the creek, but from the other side of the camp-fire. Playback started and the familiar nighttime sounds of crackling, crickets, and the creek filled the lab.

"So yeah, I decided to take first watch tonight to give Darren and Trish a break. Aside from a couple deer coming to the stream to drink I haven't seen any other animals."

There was a sudden high-pitched squeaking from above that grew louder then faded as she looked up at the partially-cloudy sky. A dark object was seen briefly darting across her field of view above. "There are a fair number of bats, though."

"Anyhow, I decided to start recording and talking be-cause...well...Trish and Darren are having sex right now."

She glanced across the campfire to the tent by the treeline that was shuddering every few moments. "They think they're being quiet, but they're really not, so I decided to just talk right now to you guys instead of listening to that."

The fire popped and she turned her head back over to the creek. "This does have me thinking, though. Trish told me a long time ago she was on the pill because her and Darren didn't want to have chil-dren. I've been on the pill before and I know how it works. If she stopped taking the pill when we came here, she'd start ovulating within a week, which is around now. Even if she brought her supply with her, eventually she's going to run out. What happens if they get pregnant?"

She picked up a stick from the ground and poked at the fire, turn-ing over a log. The entire screen turned a bright greenish-white as a flame flared up in the night vision. "And it also begs the question: if...when we find Jake, will we have kids? Would we even want to bring kids into this world? We weren't even sure if we wanted to bring kids into our world back in 2019. And without modern medi-cine and technologies, would we even have healthy children? I'm not sure if I could cope with losing a child. What was the infant mortality rate before the twentieth century? God! And here's another thing: we could only bring limited supplies with us. I'm not looking for-ward to having my period when the tampons run out!"

A short series of barely audible groans were heard from the left speakers in the lab and the camera swung back towards the tent. Sara sighed in relief. "Well, I guess they're done. Honestly, though, I'm glad they are able to find comfort in each other in this place and time. I hope Jake and I can too." She stopped the recording.

The next video series started with Sara's feed only, but right after Father Julien pressed play Trish and Darren's feeds started up. Based on the pictures in each feed, Sara was moving while crouched along an animal trail while Trish and Darren were following behind her, respectively. Trish and Darren were crouched as well.

Sara called back to them in a hushed tone. "You guys recording this?"

Trish gave a thumb's up and whispered. "Affirmative."

The trio moved cautiously ahead along the trail when a loud, low-pitched grunting noise came through the speakers in the lab. Trish and Sara froze immediately while Darren continued to creep up to Trish. "What are we thinking, ladies?"

"Could be more mastodons," Sara whispered back.

Trish looked back at Darren. "I have no idea."

In Trish's feed, Darren licked his finger and held it up in the air above his head. "We're downwind of whatever it is, so it probably doesn't know we're coming yet. Let me take point."

Both women nodded in agreement and Darren crept past them and moved further up the trail, while Sara fell back to Trish's position. The terrain that could be seen in the video feed was hilly. The trail ahead turned a corner and as Darren reached the corner it became obvious that he was at the precipice of a sinkhole. He went down on his belly and crawled up to the edge as the low-pitched grunting grew louder. He held the rifle in front of him ready to aim. His camera finally peered over the edge revealing a large, blurry dark shape moving below. As the camera came into focus an extremely large brown bear with unusually long legs came into view. It was using its front paws to roll a rotting log and every once in a while it would stop rolling the log and claw at it, putting its short, stubby snout down to lick at insects crawling on the log.

Darren watched the giant beast for a minute or two before he very carefully crawled away from the edge, and back down the trail to the women who were watching him.

"What is it?" asked Sara.

"A bear. But not like any I've ever seen. It's huge…over five feet tall on all fours. Way bigger than a grizzly. Might even give a polar bear a run for its money. Probably another one of those crazy-ass extinct giant species out here."

Trish looked at the others. "What's the plan?"

Sara was the first to speak. "With bears aren't you supposed to make a lot of noise so they know you're coming and scare them off? That's what Jake said in his video. Maybe we should yell and clap."

"That works for bears in 2019. I have no idea if this monster will be scared or curious or angered by any noise we make. Its legs were crazy long, too, which means it might be a fast runner. Even though we have the high ground most bears can climb. If we get its attention we might find ourselves on the menu."

"Can we sneak past it?" Sara asked.

Trish shrugged. "Maybe. But if we end up moving upwind of it, it might end up picking up our scents and coming for us anyway."

Darren pointed to the bend in the path ahead. "Right, and this trail definitely will put us upwind up ahead"

He looked down at the ground for a brief while then looked back up at the women. He gripped the rifle tighter and lifted it up. "I could try and take it out, though I might only be able to get one or two shots off before it was on top of me."

Trish shook her head. "It's better if we use our ammo sparingly. Once it's gone our guns become lovely door stoppers."

"Can we wait for it to leave?"

Darren grimaced as he considered the idea. "Maybe? But how long do we wait? What if it decides to come up here or the wind changes direction while we're waiting? The reality is, right now us being clustered together makes us sitting ducks. What's important is that we reach Jake. So here's my plan." He handed Trish the rifle. "Give me your piece."

Trish unholstered her pistol and gave it to him. "Trish, you take point and lead Sara down the trail past the bear, slowly. Once you guys get a couple hundred metres away, book it. I'll stay here and watch the bear to make sure it doesn't go anywhere or start following you. If it looks like you're in the clear I'll catch up to you after ten minutes."

"What? No!" Sara exclaimed in a hushed voice. "We need to stay together!"

"Look, if the bear looks like it's going to follow you guys I'll get its attention and lead it back down the trail away from you two."

"Trish! You can't seriously be considering this!"

Trish put her hand on Sara's shoulder. "It's the best plan given the circumstances. Our mission is to get you to Jake. You think you can make it if that thing comes after you, babe?"

Darren slid his backpack off. "Not with this. Take it with you. You'll need the extra supplies." As Trish held the pack he carefully unzipped it and removed a hand cranked walkie talkie. "This should allow us to keep in contact if we get separated."

"And what's the contingency plan?"

Darren clipped the walkie talkie to his belt. "You continue along this trail until you hit the next creek, lake, or river and set up camp. If I don't meet you in twenty-four hours you continue on without me."

He held out his wristwatch and Trish held out hers as they confirmed that they were synchronized.

"Roger that," Trish said as she pulled Darren into an embrace and kissed him passionately. "Be safe," she whispered in his ear.

"See you soon, babe. And remember…no matter what happens, the mission comes first. Find Jake."

He then crept ahead to where the trail got closest to the edge of the sinkhole, and the sounds of the bear became louder. He dropped to his stomach and crawled up through the brush until the bear was visible in his camera again. It was still pawing and licking at the rotting log.

From Sara and Trish's feeds, Darren could be seen gesturing for them to approach. Very carefully they made their way up to Darren, whose feet were partially on the trail from where he was laying. Trish grabbed and squeezed his right calf lovingly before moving ahead. As Sara started to pass by, Darren put his hand out for her to wait. As she paused he placed his pistol on the ground in front of him, brought his hand to his helmet and shut his camera off. The display on the screen immediately rearranged to show just Sara and Trish's feeds. From Sara's view, Darren very carefully opened the waterproof plug on his helmet camera and ejected the microSD card. He held it out to Sara who leaned forward with cupped hands to catch it as he dropped it into them. He mouthed something silently at her, and she nodded, closing her hand tightly around the tiny chip.

"What was he saying there?" the Monsignor asked.

Father Julien rewound the video a few times and the four men stared intently at Darren's mouth, each trying to mouth along with him to get an idea of the words he was saying.

"In case I don't make it," Jean-Paul said solemnly, having successfully read Darren's lips.

Father Julien resumed playback. Trish had moved further up the path and Sara crept up to her. Trish gave her a quizzical look and Sara reached out her hand and unfolded her fingers, revealing the microSD card. Trish pursed her lips and took the card, placing it in a zippered pocket. They crawled a few metres down the trail until Trish stood up, helped Sara to her feet, then started walking briskly but carefully down the trail. The terrain appeared to be sloping downhill.

For several minutes the women walked in silence and nothing but birdsong, insects buzzing, and the sound of their footfalls in the spongy terrain could be heard. All of a sudden a gunshot rang out causing both women to initially freeze. The men in the lab all jumped in their seats.

"Run!" Trish said out loud as she gestured for Sara to go ahead of her. Sara started running quickly down the trail, jumping over tree roots and moving around large rocks. Trish followed behind her, periodically slowing down to bring the rifle up and check behind them to make sure they weren't being followed. A few times Sara stumbled and fell, and Trish would pick her up by the backpack with one arm while gripping the rifle with the other and push her ahead. The Monsignor looked away from the screen again as both feeds jostled and bounced.

After several minutes of running, the women broke through the brush to yet another creek. Sara stopped at the bank and bent over putting her hands on her knees, gasping as she was out of breath. Trish put her back to Sara and pointed the rifle at the trail they had just emerged from.

"Water! We're supposed to stay here and wait for Darren, right?"

Trish didn't take her eyes off of the forest. "We aren't far away enough. We can't stay here."

"What do we do then?"

"Which way is the wind blowing?"

Sara licked her finger and held it up, then pointed downstream. "It's blowing that way."

Trish spoke very calmly. "Okay. Go get a few branches and make an arrow in front of the trail pointing in that direction. Also make a letter 'T' to put next to the arrow so when Darren gets here he knows it's ours and not one of Jake's. And be quick."

"Got it!"

Sara ran to the edge of the brush and gathered up a few sticks each around a foot long. She went back behind Trish and arranged them on the ground as Trish had instructed. "Now what?"

Trish glanced down at the marker and then took a step backwards over it. "Get in the water."

Sara took a few steps into the water which muddied around her feet. Trish stepped backwards and followed her in. "You've got point," Trish continued. "Lead us a few hundred metres down the creek. Help guide me so I keep my footing. I've got our six."

Sara put a hand on Trish's backpack and started walking downstream, looking for rocks to step on to avoid getting stuck in the mud. Trish awkwardly stepped backwards behind her, keeping the rifle trained on the trail's exit. Once they were about a dozen metres away, Trish turned and walked alongside Sara, frequently turning back to see if anything had emerged from the woods.

"So what are we doing in the creek?"

"Masking our trail. And by heading downwind, if that bear decides to follow us it'll lose our scent at the marker."

After about thirteen minutes, Sara scanned the opposite bank for a suitable location. "There," she said, pointing to an area with large rocks along the bank. "There's no animal trails nearby and there's enough of a clearing along the bank to set up camp." They left the creek and carefully walked up the rocks and back to the grass. Sara dropped to the ground to sit, panting heavily. Trish positioned herself so that she could watch upstream.

"I'm sure he made it," Sara said supportively.

"I'm sure he did, too. He's a tough son-of-a-bitch and hard to kill. In the meantime, we have to stay focused. You start setting up the tent. Once that's done I'm going to gather dry wood and get a fire going."

"Okay. We should turn our cameras off until Darren gets back."

"Agreed."

Sara's feed then stopped and after waiting a few more moments looking upstream, Trish's feed ended as well.

"I'm sure Darren made it," Father Nic said.

Father Julien advanced to the next feed, which was Trish's. The scene showed the long shadows of dusk casting across the creek. To the left was the campfire with Sara sitting on the ground beside it, holding her metal cup in her hands. Behind her was the tent. Once again the babbling sounds of the running water and the crackling of a campfire filled the lab. The rifle sat across Trish's lap, pointing away from the campsite.

"Try it again, please," Trish asked.

Sara picked up the walkie talkie on the ground next to her and pressed the call button. "Darren, this is Sara. Please come in. Over." Releasing the button, only static could be faintly heard over the sound of the creek. Sara waited a few moments and then repeated the page. Still radio silence. She put the radio back on the ground.

"Fuck! We should have tried to shoot the fucking thing. I shouldn't have been so worried about our goddamn ammo!"

"Hey. Darren said twenty-four hours. We got here in the early afternoon, so we'll stay here all day tomorrow then leave the morning after. We'll keep the campfire going; even if he misses our marker he'll see the smoke."

She got up and brought a plate of mushrooms, berries, and greens to Trish. "You should eat."

Trish ignored her. "I don't know what the fuck we were thinking. Fucking suicide mission to try and save fucking Jake when we all know he's already fucking dead. Now we're both widows."

Sara stared at the ground quietly and put the plate on the rock next to Trish. "I...I'll just leave this here." She walked away and out of the shot.

Trish shook her head a few times, brought her hand to her face and muttered "fuck". She then called out "I'm sorry!" to Sara before reaching up and ending the recording.

The next recording was Sara's feed. It was in night vision mode and as Father Julien started playback the sound of the crackling campfire could be heard.

"Trish is finally asleep. She took first watch after dusk and I got up to relieve her about thirty minutes ago. I've only done night watch that one time before...Darren and Trish always took care of it...and I can't handle the rifle so I have this bow and arrow in case any animals show up...not that I'd be much better with it. I've only practised a few times at some of our camps along the way. I'm not very good yet."

An owl's call from the woods made Sara jump. "It is freaking spooky out here." She then sat silently for a few minutes.

"Darren hasn't caught up with us yet or contacted us on the radio. I'm really worried about him and I feel terrible for Trish. This wasn't supposed to happen. All this to try and save Jake and we lose Darren to some giant extinct bear...sometimes I wonder what was I thinking? What kind of nightmare have I dragged my best friends into? I don't blame her for hating me right now, but she's all I have left."

An electronic beep suddenly sounded, barely audible over the babbling brook. "The battery on the camera is low. We forgot to charge them today." She looked up at the sky, the night vision awash in the dazzling array of tiny lights. "It's a clear night tonight so hopefully there's sunlight to recharge the cameras. If not, we'll be doing a lot of cranking." At that point the video ended.

The next video was Trish's feed, and again it was in night vision. She was sitting on the same rock as before, watching upstream. "So we spent the day charging the cameras and keeping the fire going to make sure the smoke was visible," she began. "And no, Darren didn't show up. I talked to Sara and apologized for flipping out on her. I can't believe I lost my shit like that. Darren and I knew what we were getting into and what the risks were. It's still really hard to lose the one you love and I can't help but be mad at her and Jake because of this." She sniffled, trying to keep her emotions in check. "It sucks...like really. Fucking. Sucks. But I understand now how Sara has been feeling."

She snorted loudly and brought her arm up to her face to wipe her nose on her sleeve. "However, I'm doing my best to follow my training. I'm focused on the mission. We will find Jake. We must find Jake. Darren's death in this god-forsaken place can't be for nothing."

She ended the recording.

The next video started with just Sara's feed and the initial frame revealed that it was now daytime. The tent had been packed up and the fire had been extinguished. But Sara's feed showed an arrow made out of rocks beside the first pointing upstream. As the video started Sara was just finishing arranging rocks above the arrow to show "T + S".

Sara began talking to the viewers in the lab. "In case you're wondering, we're heading back up to the nature trail we came out of when we ran away from the bear, and we'll resume heading south from there. Assuming Darren is out there and looking for us and finds this campsite, I'm leaving this here to direct him back upstream to where our previous marker was."

Trish's feed came online, revealing she was standing several metres behind Sara, further upstream. "Are you ready?"

Sara stood up and dusted her knees off. "Ready! Are you sure you're okay? We can wait another day or two."

Trish shook her head. "No. No matter what has happened, this mission must come first. We must find Jake. And when we do, we will either celebrate his rescue...or we will both mourn our lost husbands together."

Sara gave a thin-lipped smile and nodded slightly as she jogged briskly to catch up with Trish, taking a moment to wrap an arm around her and hug her. As they walked they each took turns calling out Darren's name, though Trish kept the rifle held up and pointed ahead the whole time. When they reached the animal trail they exited from, Sara crossed the creek.

"What are you doing?" Trish called.

Sara reached the marker of sticks she had made two days previously, pointing downstream. "I'm updating our note to Darren," she called back, as she picked up the three sticks that made up the arrow and rearranged them so that it was now pointing across the creek. As she started to cross the creek again to rejoin Trish, she looked further upstream and noticed a series of rocks making a straight line leading out of the water and up the bank. She pointed at them. "Look there!"

As Trish walked along the bank briskly Sara made a beeline to meet her, splashing through the creek as she moved. They both reached the rocks at the same time and standing close to them they could see that the long grass was obscuring a rock arrow pointing to an animal trail not originally visible from where its mate across the creek had exited.

"Do you think Darren missed our marker and made this one for us?" Sara said hopefully.

Trish grimaced and shook her head. "No, Darren would have added a 'D' so we could distinguish any of his markings from Jake's, just like we did."

She crouched down and picked up one of the rocks, revealing dead and white grass underneath. "Plus, these rocks have clearly been here for a few weeks; this must be one of Jake's."

"What? How is that possible? Jake stopped leaving markers once he knew he was in the past."

"Hard to say," Trish said as she stood up and surveyed the area, holding the rifle in retention. "Maybe he left it in case he got lost and walked in circles, so he'd know he'd been there before. Maybe he left it because he had gotten into the habit of creating them. Maybe he just wanted to leave something behind...a 'Jake was here' kind of sign."

Sara stood up and adjusted her backpack. "Maybe. Or maybe he was still holding out hope that someone was looking for him."

"It's still weird that we'd stumbled across his route again. We've been taking a different path from him since the fishing camp."

Sara's face twisted up in confusion. "Yeah. What are the odds?"

Trish smiled at her tight-lipped and shrugged. She took one last look up and down the creek. "Okay, let's move out. We're burning daylight."

Sara pulled out her walkie-talkie and gave it several cranks before attaching it to her belt. "I'm going to leave this on just in case."

As they stepped into the animal trail the scene grew darker as the new leaves on the canopy were providing significant shade. The forest ahead was dark. A few metres in, Trish turned her camera off and Sara's feed filled the screen, showing Trish walking ahead of her.

"We should stop recording to conserve battery life. We can start it up again if something interesting happens, if Darren finds us or contacts us, or if we find Jake's next campsite. Keep an eye open for it."

"Roger," Sara said, doing her best soldier impression. Her hand appeared in the scene briefly as she reached up and stopped the recording.

Father Nic got up and walked over to the Monsignor and Jean-Paul, holding out his tablet for them to look at. On it was a drawing of a bear that looked similar to the one the trio had encountered. "I started looking up potential candidates as soon as I saw it on the screen. It was likely a short-faced bear; *Arctodus simus*. It was one of the biggest land-dwelling carnivores that ever existed."

Jean-Paul leaned in to look at the drawing. "So what were Darren's odds of survival?"

Father Nic's face contorted with uncertainty. "The Wikipedia entry and other sites I've found so far offer contradictory information. It's hard to guess how extinct animals might have behaved."

The Monsignor nodded in understanding. "I pray he survived. In the meantime, let's resume the playback."

Sara's feed was the next one up, and the freeze frame showed a new campsite in a clearing surrounded by tall birch and oak trees, nestled in brush and ferns. Sara was standing far from the campfire where Trish was sitting and cooking over the open flames.

"We were unable to find any sign of Jake's next campsite before dusk today,so we've set up camp here in this clearing. We also haven't seen any sign of Darren, and the radio has been silent. I'm still hopeful that he's okay and he finds us."

She walked over to the fire and started talking louder. "I've made us some 'Manitoba Salad' as we've started calling it, and Trish shot a rabbit with her bow and she's cooking it up right now."

Trish rotated the carcass over the flames on a makeshift spit. "I'd like to say we're not lost but we're in completely uncharted territory on what is basically another planet compared to 2019 so we are the very definition of 'lost'. The best we can do is continue heading south to try and reach Stony Mountain. I think this is just about ready."

Sara sighed as she sat down next to Trish. "I've never eaten rabbit before nor would I ever have considered it, but right now beggars can't be choosers."

"You want a leg or a breast?" Trish asked as Sara ended the recording.

Advancing to the next frame showed Trish's feed was online, and the initial frame showed Sara standing along an animal trail in the woods with her hand up beside her head. "Camera on?" Trish said as the video started.

Sara's feed then started up and the screen split into two. "Yeah, I think so."

From Sara's viewpoint Trish could be seen further ahead, crouched. Sara crouched down and carefully made her way to Trish. In the background, between bird calls was an intermittent and very low-pitched grunting noise.

"Is it another bear?" Sara whispered.

"No idea. Let's move very slowly."

The cameras were white balanced against the darkness of the forest, but the trail they were on exited into an open, sunlit area whose brightness prevented the watchers in the lab from seeing further ahead. Trish put her arm back to keep Sara to the right edge of the path as they approached a large maple. Trish leaned her right side against the tree, retaining the rifle as she slowly stood up, wincing as she scraped her arm along the bark. Sara watched looking up from Trish's waist level as Trish quickly lowered the rifle into the crotch of a branch in the tree and took aim. She pivoted in several directions as she surveyed the opening, her feed becoming blurred and washed out by the sunlight.

"What do you see?"

Ignoring Sara, Trish pivoted a few more times before withdrawing the rifle from the tree and slinging it over her shoulder. Finally she extended a hand to Sara to help her stand up. "C'mon," Trish said, gesturing with her head in the direction of the opening.

As the two women walked out of the woods their feeds were momentarily washed out by the white light of the bright day. As the cameras adjusted another large field of prairie grass stretched out before them with a deep blue sky above, filled with flocks of birds, as usual. The source of the grunting however, was an enormous bison about ten metres from the animal trail they had just exited from.

Sara stared at the beast. "Holy shit," she exclaimed quietly.

Beyond it was a smaller cluster of six more giant bison.

"I've seen bison on farms back home," Trish said in a low voice. "But never anything this big."

Sara spoke slowly as the bison warily eyed them both. "I think these are those antique bison, or whatever they're called, that Jake photographed."

"If you're right then it's a good sign. It means we're on the right track. And these guys are safe because Jake clearly spent some time with them, given all the photos he took."

"Yeah. I wish we could stay and watch these amazing animals, but we have to keep moving."

Trish turned off her feed and started walking past the bison southward. Sara followed closely behind Trish but kept looking back at the herd. Once they had moved far enough away, Sara ended her feed as well.

The next video started with Trish's feed. The initial frame showed Sara's face, smiling. Jean-Paul noted that her cheeks were quite a bit rosier than when she was in Rome, most likely due to frequent exposure to the elements. The video started and the sound of wind filled the lab. In the sky above them grey clouds moved quickly.

"Okay, go!" Trish said off camera.

"Well, we've been continuing on for another day and a half, more or less, since the giant bison, and we've tried our best to travel due south but without any further markers from Jake we had no idea if we were heading the same way he did."

Sara started walking past Trish, who turned to keep the camera on Sara. "But I have a feeling we're back on track. Welcome..." she said, turning her body and extending her arm away from the camera with a large flourish, "...to Narcissist Park!"

As the camera focused past Sara it revealed a large open area of brush and rocks that was swarming with garter snakes. "Fuck, that just creeps me right the hell out!"

Sara grimaced at Trish. "I thought you were going to hum the theme music?"

"I never agreed to that."

"It's *Narcisse*, not narcissist," Jean-Paul said out loud.

Sara looked back at the camera. "Of course, this is likely the place that will become Narcisse, Manitoba in about ten thousand years. But it's pretty darn close to where Jake passed through a few days ago, which means we're getting closer to him. Oh, and he called it 'Narcissist' in his video so I figured I'd do a *Jurassic Park* bit. Pretty good, eh?"

The Monsignor shrugged his shoulders and tilted his head slightly. "Meh. The joke about the cougars was better."

"So how are we going to get past Jake's 'Snakes on a Plain'?" Trish asked rhetorically while holding out a long stick to Sara.

Sara took the stick and showed it off like the prize on a daytime game show. "We'll use this lovely walking stick that I've sharpened to a point here to gently move the snakes out of the way. That's what Jake did and it worked for him."

"This had better fucking work. Unfortunately we didn't take time to charge the cameras and I'm not sitting in one place by these snakes to charge them by hand, so we should stop recording here until we're clear of this nightmare."

Sara nodded. "Sounds good to me," she said just before ending the recording.

The next video feed was from Sara's camera and was in night vision mode. She was throwing a few more logs into a dying campfire and muttering "oh crap!" over and over. The sound of the embers being disturbed and the subsequent crackling filled the lab.

Sara sat back away from the fire, picked up a bow and became silent. Suddenly a new sound came over the speakers. It started quiet but grew louder and more sustained; a dire wolf was howling in the distance.

"*Merde*," Jean-Paul muttered under his breath as he straightened up in his chair.

"Shit! Trish! Trish!" Sara called in a hushed tone as she dropped the bow, scrambled to the tent, and fumbled trying to find the zipper in the dark. The howling died away.

A light came on in the tent and Trish poked her head out, half awake. "What!? What!?" Her breath was visible in the cold night air.

"Listen!"

Sara remained crouched in front of the tent staring at Trish as she turned her head to listen into the night, her eyes closed.

A few moments later another howl started up. This time it was joined by a second wolf, then a third.

Trish's eyes went wide. "Oh fuck!" she gasped. She ducked back into the tent and started to redress. "Is your jacket on?"

"Yes!" Sara replied. She nervously looked around the small clearing they were camping in and tugged on the cuffs of her sleeves to make sure they were all the way down.

Trish soon came out and joined Sara. "Get to the fire!"

Sara rushed to the fire and picked up the bow and one of the arrows she had left beside it earlier.

Trish took position on the other side of the fire with the rifle. "Not the bow, the stick! It's so dark you aren't going to see them until they're on us and a bow's no good in close quarters. Keep your back to the fire!"

Sara dropped the bow and picked up her sharpened walking stick, and turned her back to the fire, as instructed. There was quiet as Sara remained motionless, staring into the brush. Trish, having established a defensive position, took a moment to turn her camera on, and the screen split into two. Both feeds panned over the forest, though even with night mode on, nothing could be seen.

After what felt like an eternity to everyone watching, the wolves started howling again, but their call was quieter than before.

Trish lowered the rifle. "I think they're moving farther away. Are you good over there?"

"Yeah, there's nothing here."

Trish sat down on a log by the fire but kept the rifle on her lap. Sara watched her side of the forest for another minute and then joined her.

"How long before I was supposed to relieve you?"

Sara checked her watch. "Another forty-five minutes or so."

"I can take over now. You go lay down."

"I don't think I can sleep. I wouldn't want to be in the tent and unprepared if those things show up."

Trish patted the log next to her. "Then sit here with me."

Sara picked up the bow and arrow she had discarded earlier and placed them beside the log before sitting next to Trish. The wolves could be heard howling again, but the sound was very distant. She checked her watch again. "Jake was attacked a few days ago. We only have two days before he makes his last recording."

"We'll get there," Trish said reassuringly. She moved the rifle to rest on the ground beside her. Putting her arm around Sara, she guided her to lay her head down on her lap. "You should rest. If anything shows up you'll be here with me."

Sara stopped her camera feed. Trish looked down at her as she squirmed slightly to get more comfortable and hugged her stick to her chest. Trish panned the clearing's edge one last time before she turned off her camera.

The next feed was from Trish's camera, shot during the day. Sara was standing on top of a large boulder in an open area of tall grass. Trish was coming up quickly to the rock and put out her hand as Sara squatted to help pull her up as well.

Once Trish had her footing she turned to Sara. "Okay, I just started recording. Want to catch everyone up?"

Sara nodded and cleared her throat. "The wind changed direction this morning and the wolves have picked up our scent. We've seen them in the distance a couple of times and it's obvious they're coming our way. We've been basically running all day but they're still on our tail."

Sara turned on her camera, once again splitting the screen in two, and started panning the forest to the north. She suddenly stopped and amongst the trees large dark shapes could be seen darting back and forth several hundred metres away. "There they are!" she said loudly while pointing.

"If they're behaving similar to how they did in Jake's video, then they're probably doing reconnaissance in order to decide when and how best to attack," Trish said. "They could also be attempting to direct us into a preferred kill zone."

"So what's our move? Do we run?"

Trish turned as faced south. The forest was giving away to more open areas with smaller clumps of trees, prairie grasses, and distant bogs. "Negative. We're already tired from double-timing it today and we don't know what's ahead. The area is getting swampier and from here I can't see a good defensive position. We should find an open space, build a large fire, and prepare to defend ourselves. They'll probably attack when it's dark, like they did with Jake."

Trish then jumped down off the large rock and grabbed Sara's hand to help her land as she followed. They started heading southwest, away from the treelines.

"I guess we can turn our cameras off now," Sara suggested.

"Affirmative," Trish replied just before her feed ended. Sara's ended shortly afterwards.

The next video feed was Sara's, and while the picture was very dark, it was still in colour. The initial frame was looking down at an area of short plants and dirt. As it sprang to life the scene lurched forward as she picked up a bunch of loose branches from the ground and ran up to a large campfire where she tossed the branches into it. "Okay, they're in the fire!" she yelled.

Trish's feed started up and she pulled out one of the crank flashlights from her backpack and started rapidly cranking it. "Okay, so this is it. The wolves are here. They're circling our camp. We set a large fire, and we both drank a lot of water and peed at various spots near the clearing in the hopes that between the fire and us marking our territory it'd make them back off. Doesn't look like it worked, though."

She finished charging the light, turned it on and laid it down in the grass, pointing it at the woods. She then stood up and surveyed the area. It was dusk and the brightness of the campfire and not-quite-yet-black western horizon was keeping the cameras in day vision. The clearing they had set their camp up at was encircled by brush which faded quickly into foreboding shadows.

Trish looked over at Sara and pointed to a dark area of their campsite. "It's going to be pitch black soon. Get a light on that corner!" she barked as she turned back to her side of the clearing.

"On it!" Sara called back. She pulled a crank flashlight out of her backpack and started turning the handle rapidly as she ran close to the edge of the brush. Putting the light down on the ground she turned it on and aimed it at the clearing's edge, only to see the huge eyes of a dire wolf peering out at her.

Screaming, Sara fell back and started scrambling away from the wolf. Before she could turn to see what was happening, Trish saw two other wolves encroaching cautiously from the brush on her side.

"Oh fuck!" Trish said as she brandished the rifle and aimed it at the closest wolf. Before she could fire Sara screamed again and Trish turned back to see the wolf leaping into the clearing as Sara was stumbling towards her walking stick.

Trish fired at the wolf as it lunged at Sara but she missed, her shot striking the ground and kicking up dust. The wolves were clearly startled by the sound but did not retreat. Sara managed to get to her walking stick and quickly twisted her body, putting the stick between her and the wolf. Its deadly jowls clamped down on the stick, causing her to get into a tug of war with the massive canine. Sara's feed was filled with the bright white teeth of the wolf on her stick and the sound of the snarling beast was deafening. With minimal light now entering her camera, Sara's feed switched to night mode and the wolf appeared as a hellish demon in full green detail, its eyes glowing like embers.

"Help!" she called as she struggled.

Trish raised her rifle then lowered it again. "I can't get a shot!" she yelled. She ran up and used the butt of the rifle to smash the wolf in the head. It yelped and released the stick, backing away. Trish raised the rifle up like a baseball bat, pursued the wolf, and swung, connecting with the wolf's shoulder. It fell over on its side while yelping more and backed off to the clearing's edge.

"Holy shit, that was awesome!" Sara exclaimed at the site .

Trish's camera could see a second wolf emerge from the brush just behind Sara's left side. "Your nine!" she yelled.

Sara looked at her in confusion. "My what?!"

The wolf started bounding towards Sara in a serpentine fashion, as if it was chasing down a dashing rabbit.

"God damn it!" Trish yelled as she spun the rifle back into firing position. She moved close enough to Sara that the barrel was past her body and fired at the rapidly approaching wolf. The bullet passed through the wolf's hindquarters and it tumbled into the dirt, whining and thrashing, looking for the source of the injury. The percussion of the shot in such close proximity caused Sara to cry out, drop her walking stick, and cover her ears in pain.

Trish aimed again at the injured wolf and was about to make a kill shot when another wolf came out from her right side and jumped at her, clamping its jaws down on her right forearm. Yanking on it, the wolf caused the rifle to point up at the sky and discharge, and between the wolf's weight and the kickback from the rifle Trish lost her balance and fell to the ground, crying out as she dropped the rifle. The wolf started dragging her away from the fire as it thrashed its head about trying to rip off her arm.

"Sara...the gun!" she cried as she repeatedly punched at the wolf with her left hand. With the wolf filling her feed and blocking out the remaining light, Trish's camera then switched to night vision also. The lab was bathed in the green glow of both feeds as the men sat at the edge of their seats.

The injured wolf started moving towards Trish to aid its companion but Sara ran up and kicked it in the ribs, knocking it to its side, and causing it to limp quickly back towards the brush. She turned to where the rifle had landed on the other side of the campfire and saw that two more wolves had entered the clearing and were standing over it. Sara dashed towards them, crouching to pick up a still-burning log from the fire. She got between Trish and the two wolves and began swinging the burning log at them. The wolves stopped advancing but held their ground, nipping at the burning log and looking for a weakness in Sara's defences.

"The fucking gun!" Trish screamed as the wolf who still held her left arm in its jaws stepped on her chest to pin her down.

The wounded wolf doubled back and joined the other two in front of Sara. Following a strategy that was no doubt instinctual to the species, they spread out and encircled her, cutting off access to the rifle and requiring her to increase the frequency of her log swinging to keep them at bay. "I'm a little busy right now!" she screamed back, while panting heavily. "C'mon, you bastards!"

"*Madonna!*" the Monsignor exclaimed at the sight.

The sounds of the growling, snarling, and nipping of the wolves came to a sudden halt when several more gunshots were heard over the speakers. The wolf on top of Trish cried out in pain and let go of her arm. With her right arm free, Trish in one fluid motion, grabbed the hilt of her hunting knife, pulled it out of its sheath and stabbed the beast in the gut, twisting it. The wolf cried out horrifically as she shoved it onto the ground beside her.

More gunshots rang out and the wolf to Sara's right cried out in pain and ran back to the brush, leaving behind a trail of blood. With the animals now confused, Sara was able to swing the burning log and connect with the head of the wolf right in front of her, knocking it backwards and to the ground. Yelping and with fur smouldering, it got up and retreated. Sara stood there holding the burning log like a baseball bat with the one remaining wolf in front of her.

"You wanna dance, fucker?" she screamed.

The dire wolf, who was holding its injured and bleeding leg up off the ground, looked at Sara, looked back towards where its pack had retreated, looked at Sara again, then turned and limped quickly off into the brush. The sound of branches snapping grew fainter as the pack retreated further into the forest.

"I didn't think so!" Sara yelled defiantly into the darkness. Once she was sure they were gone she turned and quickly dropped to the ground beside Trish, helping her into a sitting position. "Oh, my god! Trish, are you okay?"

Trish groaned, grabbing her chest. "I'm good. You shot the wolves?"

"I didn't shoot anything."

"Then who..." Trish started to say but a snapping branch to their right caused Sara to stand up with her log in hand and Trish to roll over to the rifle, pick it up, and get up on her knees into a firing position in under two seconds. They both peered into the darkness where the gunshots had come from, and while they couldn't quite make out the figure standing there, the watchers in the lab saw everything clear as day thanks to the night vision. Before them, holding a smoking pistol, was Darren. Even in the otherworldly green-tinted view it was obvious that he was bruised and bloodied.

"Darren! Yes!" cried Father Nic.

"*Sia lodato Dio!*" the Monsignor exclaimed.

"*Tabernac,*" Jean-Paul uttered impressively under his breath.

"I want to say something badass right now, but all I can think of is 'it's just been revoked'," Darren called out, doing his best impression of a tough guy from an action film.

"Darren?" Trish asked hesitantly. She lowered the rifle, got up, and started running up to him. "Darren!" She cried joyously as she embraced him tightly and started kissing him over and over again. "Oh my god! I thought I lost you!"

Sara ran up behind her, paused after the first few kisses, then moved in and hugged the both of them at the same time.

Darren grabbed Trish's face in his hands and looked her body over. "Are you okay?"

"I am now," Trish sobbed.

"But that wolf was right fucking on top you!"

"I'm fine. Just a little bruised. It's a good thing we brought these jackets. Seeing how those wolves attacked Jake in his videos gave us an edge. Its teeth couldn't get through the armour."

"Thank you army-fucking-surplus," Darren sighed while nodding his head approvingly. He looked over at Sara briefly before meeting Trish's eyes again. "Sara? You okay?"

"So much better now that you're here!" Sara exclaimed with joy as the couple resumed kissing.

Trish then stopped kissing Darren and gave him a shove backwards. "What the hell?! Where have you been? I thought you were dead!"

Darren chuckled. "Long story. Let's secure the perimeter first. And can I have my rifle back? This pistol sucks."

Trish wiped tears from her eyes and nodded, straightening herself up and going back into soldier mode. "Roger that," she said happily, and traded weapons with Darren. After holstering her pistol she reached into her pocket and pulled out the microSD card that Darren had given Sara. She reached up and inserted it back into his camera and started it recording. The screen split once again into three feeds. From Darren's feed Sara's face was again visible, her cheeks wet from tears of joy.

Trish then approached the wounded wolf on the ground. It was breathing shallowly and seemed unable to move, though its legs were twitching slightly. She pulled her hunting blade from its gut and with a quick movement she slit its throat. Dark blood started spilling out onto the moonlit rocks. "We should skin it and smoke the meat," she called to the group in a contemptuous tone.

While Trish went to work, Darren and Sara quickly visited each crank flashlight and cranked them again to charge them back up. Then with Darren standing watch Sara gathered more firewood and sat back at the campfire to stoke it. Once Sara was safely sitting at the fire holding her sharpened stick and hunting knife, Darren walked up behind Trish and retained the shotgun while she set about dressing the animal. His camera feed showed him scanning the brushline.

"Are you sure you're okay, Sara?" Darren called without turning from the bushes.

Sara called back loudly. "Yeah, though I can't really hear all that well. My ears are still ringing from all the gunfire."

"Yeah that'll pass in a while," Trish said loudly as she began cutting the pelt off the wolf. "It was a bit like Canada Day there for a moment."

Darren turned to Sara who was sitting by the fire and rubbing her ears. Suddenly she stopped, slowly lowered her hands to her lap and looked straight ahead, the expression on her face turning to one of shock.

Darren looked rapidly between the brush and Sara, trying to see what she was looking at. "What is it?"

"Fireworks," Sara said, her voice getting louder as she spoke. "Jake said he thought he heard fireworks in his last video!"

Trish stopped working on the wolf and turned to Sara. "Oh...my...God! The gunfire...it was us!" she exclaimed in realization.

"What? I don't get it—" Darren started to say.

Sara stood up and cupped her hands to her mouth. "Jake! Jake!" she called out repeatedly.

Darren hurried over to Sara and pulled her hands from her mouth. "Whoah! Whoah! Keep it down! What are you doing?"

She pulled away from Darren. "It's Jake! He heard fireworks in his last video...that was us, just now, with the guns! He's close by! JAKE! JAKE!"

Darren again grabbed her hands. "Sara, listen! A gun's report can travel far under the right conditions so he's probably still too far away to hear our voices. Even if he is, it's too dark for any of us to travel safely! We'll find him in the morning."

Trish resumed working on the wolf. "He's right. The wolves are gone for now but God knows what else is out there and we don't need to lure them right to us. Don't forget about the sabre-toothed cat!"

"Actually, assuming they're lone hunters, the sabre tooth cat from Jake's video probably won't be out hunting for a few days, given that it just had a fresh kill," Darren said.

The women both stopped what they were doing and stared at him. "What?" he said defensively. "I can know stuff too, you know. I happen to like big cats. I'm more worried about those giant beavers, though, because we know nothing about them!"

Sara started crying. "So what do we do? He's out there right now!"

Darren placed his hands on her shoulders and turned her to face him. "Look, you're in shock from the wolf attack. You need to rest...hell, we all do, and at first light we'll go find him. Besides, I've spent the last day and a half pushing hard to catch up to you guys. I need a break."

"I don't think I can sleep," Sara said between tears.

"That's fine. I'm not sure I can either. We can just hang out and talk for a bit." Darren pulled out a hip flask from inside his jacket. He unscrewed the cap and offered it to Sara. "And maybe...we can get a little buzz going."

Without hesitation Sara reached out and took the flask and took a large swig from it. "Easy now," Darren cautioned. "That's the good stuff from back home and there isn't much of it left."

Sara spoke hoarsely after taking another quick sip before handing it back to Darren and wiping her mouth with the back of her hand. "Well then, Trish better get her ass over here and get in on this before it's all gone!"

"Be right there. I'll finish up with the wolf first and then I'll cook up some of its meat."

"We might as well turn off the cameras and save the batteries," Darren suggested. With no objections Darren's feed ended first, followed shortly by Sara's, then Trish's.

Without missing a beat Father Julien advanced to the next set and hit play. The next feed started up with only Sara's stream initially. Night mode was still on, but the entire picture was washed out and completely white.

"...ait wait wait! We need to get this on video!" Sara laughed. The picture came into focus and revealed that her camera was pointed at the roaring campfire. As Sara looked up Trish was seen sitting on a log to Sara's left, holding a piece of wolf meat over the fire. It was impaled on a small stick that had been sharpened into a skewer. Standing next to Trish was Darren. Trish started her camera shortly after and the screen split in two.

"All right, now tell us where you've been," Trish said as she watched the meat she was slowly rotating. "What happened with that motherfucking monster bear? I thought it had shit you out somewhere in the woods days ago."

Darren crouched down to reenact the scene as he began his tale. "Okay...so a few minutes after you guys left the bear started sniffing the air and I realized it had picked up your scent. So I'm down there trying to figure out what to do, when this motherfucker stands up on its hind legs. It was so huge...I shit you not...even though it was down in that pit, and I'm talking like ten feet down, it's face was level with mine."

"Jesus," Sara gasped, bringing a hand to her mouth.

He stood up, mimicking the upright posture of a bear. "So the bear is suddenly looking me in the eye and both of us freak out."

Darren jumped slightly into the air, raising his arms. "So I jump up and raise my arms, trying to make myself bigger, and talking loud, like you're supposed to do with bears. But of course this thing has never seen a human before, and it's huge so it backs up and starts running towards my side of the sinkhole. I backed the fuck up and the fucking thing got a paw up on the trail on its first jump."

"Holy shit," Trish exclaimed. "What'd you do?"

"I turned and I booked it. Straight back down the trail the way we came, like a bat outta Hell, to lead it away from you guys. I kept running and running for a really long time, but I could hear this thing crashing through the bushes behind me the whole way! So at one point I turned and aimed the pistol and fired!"

He pantomimed holding a gun and pulling the trigger.

"We heard the shot," Sara said. "Did you hit it?"

"Not even close. The bear wasn't as close as I thought, I had your shitty handgun, and I wasn't exactly at my steadiest. But, it did make the bear stop for a moment. So I took that opportunity to run off the path into the thicker bush. There was a large tree up ahead that looked like I could climb quickly."

Trish clicked her tongue at him. "You're not supposed to climb trees when a bear is chasing you, stupid."

"I know that. But this bear was so huge I figured it wouldn't be able to climb."

"So you climbed it anyway?" Sara asked incredulously.

"What the hell else was I gonna do? I couldn't outrun the bastard."

"So you got your ass up a tree?" Trish asked.

"Damn skippy," Darren boasted as he mimed climbing a tree. "Pretty sure I set a world record."

"What did the bear do?" Sara asked impatiently.

"I'm getting to that," Darren snapped as he playfully grimaced at her. "The bear must've been really hungry for man meat because it tried to get up the tree, but as I figured it was too big to climb."

He then mimicked the bear standing on hind legs again. "So this asshole stands up and starts shaking the tree, trying to get me out. I damn near thought it was going to rip the tree right out of the ground, roots and all! I had to hang on for dear life. Of course, with all that shaking, the radio fell off my belt and landed on the ground. The bear saw it, grabbed it, and had a very unpleasant snack. So my walkie talkie was fucked."

"*That's* why you never answered us on the radio," Trish said.

"Yeah," Darren replied.

"So then what happened?" Sara asked.

"Well this bear can't get to me and I figure it's going to leave, but it doesn't. It just hangs around at the bottom of the tree waiting. I tried yelling, I tried throwing branches at it, I even took a piss in its direction...didn't hit it, though. It just wouldn't go away. I waited until dusk and eventually I was so exhausted that I fell asleep holding onto the tree."

"No way!" Trish exclaimed.

Darren raised his hand into a boy scout salute. "Scout's honour, like a goddamn monkey. I don't know how long I slept but when I woke up it was late afternoon and I damn near fell out of the tree because I didn't know where I was at first."

"And the bear?" Sara asked.

"Gone. It must have left during the night. Though I waited a long time before making my way down. Of course being the idiot that I am I jumped out of the tree from too high and ended up spraining my ankle. I couldn't find the trail we were originally on so now I had to try and catch up with you, and my ankle slowed me down for the first day. I just kept moving south, but I was completely lost. I started hearing the wolves howling at night and I figured they were tracking me and that I was completely fucked. But this morning the wind changed and started blowing up from the south. By the afternoon I could smell your campfire in the wind so I followed my nose until I saw the firelight from a few klicks away and finally caught up with you."

"And not a moment too soon!" Sara exclaimed.

Darren sat down next to Trish. "Wow, babe, that is one crazy story."

Sara tossed another log on the fire and a stream of embers was sent up into the sky.

"That was a smart idea, grabbing the burning log and using it to keep the wolves back," Trish said to her.

"Thanks," Sara said. She then paused and a look of realization came across her face.

"What is it?" Darren asked.

"Fire! We should have used fire to try and scare the bear away! Why didn't we think of that?"

Sara looked over at Darren and Trish, who were contemplating her revelation. Darren rubbed the stubble on his chin. "Huh, I don't know. I guess I never really consider fire when dealing with wild animals... probably out of concern over starting a forest fire or something."

"Well we'll remember it for next time," Trish said as she shook her head.

Darren leaned over as close as he could and sniffed at the meat on the stick. "How's dinner coming?"

She took the stick and jabbed it into the ground, creating a small pike holding the meat up. She pulled out her knife, cut off a chunk, and handed it to Darren. "Looks like it's pretty cooked. Try some."

Darren sniffed it then took a bite and chewed it for a few minutes. "Ugh, I guess this is like eating dog. It's really chewy...but you know, it's not that bad. Whatever we need to do to survive."

They sat quietly for a few minutes while Darren ate the meat. Trish had her arm around him and Sara sat staring into the fire.

Sara was the one who broke the silence. "This. This is humanity right here."

"What are you talking about?" Darren said as he loudly swallowed.

"Well think about it...for most of human history people sat around fires, shared meals, and told stories. Despite all our creature comforts and technology, if you take it all away, this is what we fall back on. Every human alive right now, in this time, is doing exactly this."

Darren and Trish nodded silently. Trish pulled her arm out from behind Darren and grabbed his and Sara's hands. "No matter how far we've come, as long as we're together, this is home. We are a tribe now." They all smiled at each other.

"Can I have some more dog, please?" Darren asked, ruining the moment. The women laughed.

"You know what, I'll try the bastard too," Sara announced bravely. "Frickin' thing tried to take a bite out of us; let's take a bite out of it."

Trish cut up more pieces of the meat and gave them to Sara before cutting some off for herself. Sara started chewing but quickly started looking revulsed.

"Mmmph! This has quite a distinct taste to it!"

Trish agreed, chewing loudly. "Yeah. It's not like beef or pork...but kind of like venison."

"Well, we're the first humans in ten thousand years to eat dire wolf," Darren said proudly, "and I can't wait to add mammoth to that list!"

"Mastodon!" Sara and Trish said in unison, their mouths full.

"Whatever," Darren groaned, rolling his eyes.

Sara swallowed the food in her mouth. "Mammoth wouldn't be as big of an accomplishment as you'd think"

"How's that?" Trish asked.

"A bunch of scientists like a hundred years ago found a frozen mammoth in Siberia and cooked and ate the meat."

"What?" Darren said incredulously. "That doesn't sound real."

"Yeah, I read it online. I did some research the week before we arrived here."

Trish rolled her eyes. "Well then, if it was online, it's definitely true."

Darren stood up. "Let's finish up here and get some rest. It's probably after midnight and we'll want to leave at first light. I'll take first watch."

The women nodded at him in agreement and his feed ended, followed shortly by Trish's, then Sara's.

When the next video started it was Darren's feed and it was still at night. He was sitting close to the fire holding the rifle across his lap. Several sticks and branches were at his feet and he picked one up and tossed it into the flames. He sighed quietly as he watched the embers float up and vanish into the starry sky.

"I guess you thought you'd seen the last of me, eh? I'll have to keep it short tonight because my camera's battery hasn't been charged for a few days, but I also haven't used it for a few days, so it's still got a bit of juice."

He panned the brush. "I'm going to try and keep watch the entire night. Sara and Trish need to recover from their encounter with the wolves. Especially Sara. Trish and I have our experiences as soldiers to be able to take the stress a bit better. I haven't slept much over the last few days but I'm still coming off the high of finding them and dealing with those wolves so I'm not overly tired right now."

"Hey, everything okay?"

Darren looked over and saw Trish standing in her sleeping attire of shorts and tank top. She wore her flak jacket over her skimpy ensemble.

"Oh yeah. Everything's good. Just talking to the future. Sorry if I woke you."

"No, it wasn't that. I woke up and just had to come out and make sure you were here and that I wasn't just dreaming that you came back."

He reached out and she took his hand as he pulled her close and embraced her. Her lips trembled. "Don't ever fucking do that to me again...I can live anywhere, in any time, but I can't live in a world without you."

"Never again, babe," he replied as he brushed a strand of hair off her face. "But even when you thought I was dead you continued on with Sara...and look how far you got! I'm so proud of you."

She wiped her nose with her sleeve. "The mission comes first." She looked around the perimeter of the clearing. "Any sign of the wolves?"

"Nah, I have a feeling they've just learned to avoid humans. Tomorrow we push into the marsh to try and get to Stony Mountain. If Jake really heard our gunshots then he can't be that far away."

"Well we haven't seen Stony yet. But we must be close to the marsh based on the terrain. Hopefully tomorrow we'll get our bearings."

A small beeping sound was heard. "My camera's about to shut off," Darren said. "I didn't get a chance to charge it while I was playing with my pet bear."

"That's okay. I've got something else for you to play with," Trish said seductively as she straddled his lap, her body filling the feed. She reached out to his helmet and stopped the recording.

The next feed was Trish's. It was daytime and Sara's face filled the screen. Upon playback Sara reached up and turned on her camera, causing the screen to divide into the two feeds. In Sara's feed

Darren and Trish could be seen standing together, a grove of poplar and birch further back behind them. Darren's feed came on next.

Sara smiled into the two cameras. "We spent some time this morning charging up our cameras before breaking camp even though I really wanted to hurry up and keep moving. It turns out that we had no idea how close we were...and now here we are."

Sara turned around. The familiar sight of bulrushes, water, and millions upon millions of birds appeared on the screen.

"They found Oak Hammock Marsh!" Jean-Paul happily exclaimed.

"Technically it was called St. Andrew's Bog. European settlers drained it all for farmland until only the modern marsh remained," Father Nic corrected him as he read from his tablet.

"Where do we go now? Where's Stony Mountain?" Trish asked.

"It's gotta be somewhere south of here," Darren said. "We're probably still too far away to see it. Remember Jake said that the original marsh extended almost to Teulon."

Everyone stood looking at the great expanse of nature before them. Sara's feed followed the north edge of the marsh until she spotted something familiar in the east. "Look there!" she called out as she started running. The others followed her, all three feeds becoming blurry from the cameras jostling.

As Darren and Trish caught up with Sara they saw a fire pit on the ground. "How'd you see the fire pit from way back there?" Darren asked as he caught his breath.

"Not the fire pit...this!"

Sara ran up to the large solitary oak tree near the marsh's edge and started climbing its branches. The Monsignor looked away from Sara's feed as it rapidly shook and panned around as she ascended but once it settled they were now looking at the same view Jake had provided them with when he had found the tree. And looking towards the southwest the same dark mound rose up just above the horizon.

She pointed in the direction of the mound. "I see Stony Mountain!" Quickly scurrying down the tree she started running towards the closest path between the bogs that went in that direction. Darren and Trish followed after her.

Suddenly a low-pitched clicking and a cow-like moaning sound overpowered the cacophony of the wetlands sounds flooding the laboratory and Sara stopped in her tracks. Ambling out of the bog only ten feet or so in front of her was one of the giant beavers. Darren and Trish caught up to Sara and each of them grabbed one of her arms and pulled her back as they retreated from the beast.

The giant beaver stopped, turned its head, and looked at the humans, its giant front teeth bared menacingly. It was so close the camera microphones had picked up its heavy breathing.

"Oh, fuck!" Darren exclaimed as the group froze.

The beaver continued to make its whining and clicking noises but after a few moments turned back to face the way it was heading and finished crossing the path, entering the water on the other side.

Father Nic pointed excitedly at the screen. "Did you see the tail? It was long but wasn't flat like a modern beaver tail!"

"So?" Jean-Paul asked.

"No giant beaver tails have ever survived to modern times because they're soft tissue! Now we know what they look like!"

"Holy shit," Sara said under her breath as the brown giant swam away from the group, looking like a dark island meandering through the marsh.

"We need to fucking avoid those things," Trish said.

Sara nodded slowly, not taking her eyes off the creature. "Agreed."

"No more running," Darren ordered. He then went around the women and started leading them down the path. Sara followed Darren, and Trish took up the rear, frequently checking behind them, her pistol in hand.

After a few minutes of following the winding animal trail, Darren put his fist up to stop the others. "Looks like there's just a lot more of this ahead. Let's kill the cameras and save it for when we reach Jake. We'll move as fast as we can."

"Okay," Sara said, turning off her feed. The other two feeds ended shortly afterwards.

The next series started with Darren's feed. As it came to life, it revealed that Darren was walking along another animal trail, deeper in the marsh. The plants lining it were quite tall, and were a mix of various aquatic plants, deer grass, and Saskatoon bushes. Dozens of small birds like chickadees and wrens flitted back and forth between the bushes on either side of the path ahead of him, while large flocks of waterfowl flew high overhead in the deep blue sky.

"I think I saw something ahead," he said. "We just have to get a bit higher."

"Trish, get up on Darren's back," Sara said from off camera.

"Oooh, good idea," Trish said as she turned on her camera. The screen was once again divided in two. "Take off your backpack, babe."

Sara helped Trish get up onto Darren's shoulders as he crouched, then helped steady Darren as he straightened up, hoisting the petite Filipina and her camera above the deer grass. At her new height, she could see a small grassy mound not far from their location, but further in the distance a familiar rocky outcrop.

"Okay, let me down," she called. Darren crouched and Sara helped her off his back. Trish recovered her backpack and moved briskly ahead. "Follow me!"

Darren got Sara to go ahead of him as picked up his backpack and followed from behind. Trish was the first to reach the small mound and its summit. As Sara joined her Trish pointed off to the south. About a kilometre away was the rocky outcrop where Jake had been attacked. Further away in the distance was Stony Mountain, noticeably larger than when Sara first saw it from the oak tree.

"Holy shit!" Sara exclaimed. "We're almost there! Let's get to Jake!"

"Not so fast," Darren cautioned. "It's already late afternoon and given how these trails wind through the marsh it might take us close to an hour to reach that outcrop. When Jake was there he said it took another six to eight hours to reach Stony Mountain. We can't make it to Stony before nightfall and we can't move through the marsh safely at night."

"Darren's right. Besides, that spot is a very defensible position if anything decides to show up."

"Okay, okay," Sara relented. "What's our fastest path there?"

Darren pointed to a barely visible depression in the foliage that served as an indication of an animal trail. "That one. Let's head out. Carefully...and cameras off."

Darren's feed ended and he and Sara started walking towards the animal trail as Trish took one last look behind them before ending her recording.

Father Julien advanced to the next set of videos and clicked play. Darren's feed filled the screen as he exited the animal trail onto the gravel-covered clearing in front of the outcrop where Jake was attacked. Trish and Sara's cameras turned on almost immediately afterwards following him into the clearing.

"We're here," he announced.

They slowly made their way to Jake's fire pit, stepping into shadows stretching long from the west as the sun was approaching the horizon. Dark bloodstains were visible over many of the rocks. Some was the blood of the dire wolf that was killed by the smilodon, and some was Jake's. As she surveyed the site Sara broke down crying. Trish walked up and grabbed her shoulders, looking her in the eyes.

"Remember, Jake survived this. We have to stay focussed on making it to Stony tomorrow."

Right," sniffed Sara. "I know. What do I need to do?"

"You and I will gather firewood while Darren pitches the tent against the outcropping and digs a latrine close by. You can do this. Right?"

Sara nodded. "Yeah. I've got this. Let's go. The sooner we get set up the sooner we sleep and the sooner we find Jake." She turned off her feed.

Trish followed Sara to a section of brushline away from the bloodstains. "Babe, we're going to get some wood from over here," she called to Darren as she turned her camera off. Darren's feed now filled the screen.

"Roger that," Darren called back as he walked up to the fire pit. He began kicking the bloodstained gravel aside to clean up the area near the fire so they could use it. "I don't know how the fuck you could have survived this shitshow, Jake, but you'd better be there tomorrow."

His feed ended.

The next feed was in night vision mode, and was from Darren's camera again. The initial frame was of the night sky; once again a dazzling array of bright points against a green background. As playback started the stars began twinkling.

"Well future people, we're at the last leg of this journey. I'm doing the whole watch tonight. If we find Jake tomorrow, and if he's alive, Trish will need to be at the top of her medical game so she needs a full night's rest. Sara was pretty shook by the mess here and could use a good night's sleep, too."

He looked at the small precipice above the tent and the campfire before panning across the brush. "It's been really quiet tonight, which I gotta admit is a nice change of pace. It's kind of crazy thinking that tomorrow we'll get to Stony Mountain and find Jake, dead or alive. The mission will be over. But what next? Where do we go from here?"

The sound of gravel being stepped on made him quickly spin and look up at the ridge. Walking up to the edge was the smilodon, its massive teeth glistening in the night vision.

"Holy fuck!"

Darren slowly raised the rifle at the giant cat. The smilodon looked over the campsite with its crackling fire, then looked over at Darren. It watched him for a few moments before it yawned, licked its lips, then turned and walked back to where it came, disappearing into the darkness.

Darren held his position for a few minutes while only the sound of the crickets and bat calls could be heard. Eventually he lowered the rifle onto his lap and exhaled deeply. He looked down at the ground for a bit and then back up at the stars. Once again the lab was filled with thousands of specks of light on the screen.

"I don't know what's going to happen after tomorrow. But I know it sure as Hell won't be boring."

He reached up and stopped the recording.

The next feed was Trish's. The first rays of sunlight fell on the gravel from the east as she looked over at Sara and Darren, who were finishing packing their backpacks. "Okay, we're ready, yes?"

"Ready," Sara said, slinging hers onto her back.

Darren stood up, picking the rifle up off the ground beside him. "I'm good to go, too."

Trish looked out to the mound noticeably rising above the southern horizon. Its eastern edge was lit by the rising sun and the green of the trees on it was visible for the first time. "Now Jake said it took him six to eight hours to get to Stony Mountain from here. But...he was injured and had lost a fair bit of blood. We're going to be faster and we're not stopping today until we get to Stony. Agreed?"

"Agreed," the others said in unison.

"Okay, I'm turning off the camera now and we're heading to Jake. We'll save our batteries for when we find him."

The video feed ended.

Father Julien swallowed hard as he started the next series. It was Sara's feed first, the initial frame looking at the base of a large hill covered in brush and rocks. Shortly after playback started Trish and Darren's cameras turned on, and the screen split again.

"Jake! Jake!" Sara started calling out as she scrambled up the escarpment before her. Darren and Trish followed closely behind and started calling out for him as well.

They clambered up the slope to the top of Stony Mountain, continuing to call for him. They reached a large tree at the top amidst long grasses and stopped, catching their breath from the climb while they listened for any response to their calls.

"Thats..." Jean-Paul started to say as his eyes widened.

"This is the tree that Jake filmed the panorama from!" Sara exclaimed between gasps. "He must be here!"

They fanned out over the hilltop, each feed showing them heading in a different direction. Darren stayed by the tree, looking out over the plain to the south. Sara moved along the southern edge through brambles and small trees. It was Trish along the northern side that was the first to spot the orange of Jake's vest in the grass.

"I've got him!" she cried as she started running. The men watching all gasped as Jake was once again on the screen. He was lying motionless next to an extinguished campfire, his skin pallid. Darren and Sara turned towards her and converged on her location. Trish reached out and grabbed Jake's wrist.

When she caught up to them, Sara dropped to her knees and slid up to Jake, picking his head up into her arms. He didn't move. "Jake! Jake! Please don't be dead!"

"He's got a pulse but it's weak," Trish said hopefully. She placed her wrist on his forehead. "He's running a really high fever."

Startling everyone in the video and the lab, Jake coughed and groaned slightly.

"*Mon Dieu*! He is alive!" Jean-Paul gasped.

Sara laughed through her tears. Trish went into field medic mode, dumped her backpack onto the ground beside her, and started pulling out and sorting medical supplies. She quickly produced a syringe and a vial, primed it, and after swabbing his arm with an alcohol wipe injected it into Jake's arm. "This is a high-dose cocktail of the strongest antibiotics from 2019," she said as she pushed the plunger in.

"Oh Jake—" Sara sobbed as she held him and rocked back and forth, kissing his forehead repeatedly.

Darren stood overlooking the situation. "What now?"

"Now we make him comfortable and let the drugs do the trick. Get a fire going and get some fresh water here. We'll make a cold compress to help bring down the fever. Hopefully it isn't too late. We might as well turn the cameras off here. The next few hours are going to be tricky."

Trish and Darren's camera feeds ended. Sara's feed stayed on as she refused to let go of Jake. Trish reached over to her and stopped her camera.

"Please don't tell me that was the last file," Jean-Paul said, turning to the Monsignor. The Monsignor, eyes watery, shrugged and looked over at Father Julien. Father Nic turned as well.

Father Julien swallowed hard and hit the right arrow as everyone turned back to the screen. Only one video appeared in the top left corner, paused on a black frame. He pressed play and the software automatically filled the screen with the one feed.

The familiar sound of wind and insects buzzing filled the room as the picture jostled and the camera was lifted, revealing that it had been resting on someone's lap. It paused briefly as Sara could be heard saying "Are you ready?"

A moment later the camera angled up. Bright sunlight flooded the lens and washed out the image, taking a second or two to adjust before the viewers were gazing once more on the face of Jacob Taylor. He was sitting on the ground, propped up against a log. He was clean-shaven and the colour had mostly returned to his face, which bore a wide smile along with a few bandages.

"Ok, go," Sara said off camera.

"My name is Jacob Taylor—" His voice was weak, but stronger than the final recording they had watched a few weeks ago. "—and I have travelled back in time about ten thousand years. I'm joined here by my best friend Darren—"

The camera swung over to Darren, who was building a teepee frame out of long branches. Darren paused his work, smiled and waved at the camera.

"—his wife Trish—"

The camera swung over to Trish who was sitting on another log and stitching together the wolf pelt into some sort of article of clothing. She looked up and smiled softly. On the ground beside her were several solar panels charging the other cameras.

"—and of course, my amazing wife Sara," he finished as Sara turned the camera on herself and smiled and waved with her free hand. Jean-Paul noticed that she looked completely different than when he last saw her. Her face was filled with happiness, and she somehow looked younger. She turned the camera back on Jake.

"I sent a message to the future via my phone which, through nothing short of a miracle, survived to 2019. And because of it my wife, my best friend, and his wife risked their lives to save mine. They got here four days ago…in the nick of time I might add…and have been caring for me ever since."

He held up his now-bandaged arm where the dire wolf had bit him. "It's already healing, and I've got a lot of my strength back. So I wanted to make sure I thanked the people who made it possible. Jean-Paul, Father Nic, Father Julien, and Monsignor...Monsignor..."

"Wowchuk," Sara interjected helpfully.

"Yes! Wowchuk!" Jake said, laughing. "Thank you all so much, and God bless you!"

Sara handed the camera over to Jake who pointed it back at her. She held up a small metal case about the size of the clay brick that Jake had made. "We will be placing all our recordings made thus far into this case. It's airtight, watertight, thermodynamically insulated, and electrically insulated. It has a titanium shell, so it's built to last. All the MicroSD cards will be going into an anti-static bag inside the case and then we'll be locking it. You'll need twentieth-century tools to open it, so hopefully nobody tries to get into it before the Vatican does."

"You forgot about the engraving," Trish said off camera.

"Oh, right." She held the box up to the camera. Engraved on the lid was the same message as Jake's brick, along with a cross and an ichthys, except with an "OPEN ON" date of June 6th, 2019.

"Don't mess with a formula that works, right? We picked a few days after we planned to leave in case you wonder where we all vanished to.

"We're also including this:" She held up a small business card-size piece of metal that glistened in the sunlight. "You might not see it in the camera, but it's a small sheet of gold-plated nickel with all your names engraved on it. Just to make sure it gets to the right people."

The Monsignor handed the aged and tarnished gold plaque, now sealed in a plastic bag, to Jean-Paul. Jean-Paul looked down and read the engraving: "For Monsignor Wowchuk, Father Nic, Father Julien, and Jean-Paul Ducharme. You'll know what to do with this."

The Monsignor smiled as he put a hand on Jean-Paul's shoulder. "Like I said, you were invited."

"Okay...my turn," Jake said as he returned the camera to Sara who pointed it back at him. "I guess you're all wondering what we're going to do now, right? Darren?"

Sara panned the camera over to Darren, who stopped working on his teepee. "Jake's original plan was sound; head south. Try to get away from the harsh winter weather and with luck, find other humans."

Jake popped back into the frame. "Oh, about that! Tell them what you saw!"

Darren reached into his backpack and pulled out his collapsible telescope, extending it for the camera. "Yesterday evening, just before sunset I was scanning the horizon with the telescope and about south, south-west I saw what appeared to be a small wisp of smoke at the horizon. It could be almost a hundred kilometres from here."

Jake popped back into the scene. "But," he said in a drawn out fashion with an upward inflection at the end. "There's a chance it could be a campfire!"

"Slow down, pardner. If there are people out there, we'll do a recon mission, first. With our surveillance tech we ought to be able to learn a bit about them before we attempt to make initial contact. We don't know this territory and we won't know these people."

Sara pulled out two more cases and put them next to the first one. They looked identical, including the markings, except one case was marked to be opened on June 8th, 2019 and the other June 10th, 2019.

"We have a LOT more MicroSD cards with us. We're going to bury this first batch in Jake's inukshuk. But we're going to keep recording as much video, audio, and taking as many photos as possible for as long as we can. As we fill up the memory cards we'll put them into this case," she explained, tapping on the first box.

She crouched down and picked up one of the boxes. "In a year's time, wherever we are, we'll build a similar inukshuk on high ground and bury the first case. Hopefully we'll find other landmarks we recognize that will still be there in 2019."

Jake turned the camera back on himself. "We've also decided that the last surviving member of this group will bury the last case. Hopefully that'll be in 30 or 40 years. But if something goes wrong and we're killed by weather, or wild animals, or hell...even other humans...these cases are built to survive."

"And we've marked them to be open over three different dates so if you find them you know what order to open them in!" Sara said loudly off camera.

Jake walked over to the cairn and pointed the camera at it. "Okay, we're getting ready to seal up the Stony Mountain inukshuk. Then tomorrow morning we're breaking camp and heading in the direction of the smoke. Hopefully we'll know if there are other people here in a couple of days."

"Four or five days, depending on the terrain," Darren corrected from off-camera.

"Whatever. Okay, I guess that's everything, then," Jake said as the feed ended.

Instinctively, Father Julien hit next. Another video appeared with its initial frozen frame showing Trish's face with her hand stretched to the camera.

"There's more?" the Monsignor said in surprise.

When playback began, she pulled her hand away and leaned back. She was sitting on a log somewhere near the large oak tree, with the scenery behind her revealing the same vista that Jake had filmed on his phone. Large dark shapes moved slowly through the prairie in the distance.

"Jake asked each of us to record a farewell message before we seal up the case and Jake's brick. So I guess this is my last confessional. I don't really know what to say here, but I think I'd kick myself if I didn't at least try to say something."

She sat for a few minutes, staring off into space as her face became serious. "I once read a poem in high school...I can't remember how it goes, about a finger that writes and moves on or something...but it's about how you can't change the past no matter how hard you try. So maybe this is fate. Jake did hear our gunshots after all, maybe we were always meant to come back here. And be stuck here."

She looked off screen, smiled, and looked back at the camera. "And given who I'm stuck here with...I think I'm going to be okay with that. I guess that's all I really have to say." She leaned forward to stop the recording. "Goodbye," she said smiling as the video came to an end.

Father Julien advanced to the next video and hit play. It was now Darren's turn, and he was sitting in the same spot Trish had been. The background looked like it hadn't changed much, suggesting that Darren had made this recording shortly after Trish's.

"So I guess this is it. Normally in movies this is the part where somebody says something really profound and inspiring. But that's not me."

He chuckled a bit and then his face became more serious. "You know, I spent a good chunk of my life serving my country. And in doing my duty I've seen good men die...on both sides. And all for what? Fighting for the quote-unquote freedom of my fellow Canadians? Bullshit. But here...now...this is the first time I felt like I've actually fought for someone's life. And it's the first time I've ever felt truly free. This place, this time...is basically Eden. No wars, no crime, no pollution, no corruption. Just life. And I know it's not going to be easy, but hey, life never is. I also know I could have stayed home and left Jake to his fate, but I'm one hundred percent certain that this was the right choice."

He looked down pensively at the ground for a few seconds before looking back up at the camera. "I guess this is it. Oh, I said that already, didn't I? Well then I suppose I should end this with something worthy of playback ten thousand years from now." He straightened himself up, crossed his arms and proudly announced "My name is Darren Reichert, and I fucking shot a dire wolf!"

Smiling, he leaned forward and stopped the recording.

Next up was Sara's video. As it started up Jean-Paul couldn't help but be struck by the difference between this woman and the woman he shared a cab with a few weeks ago.

"This feels like a dream. My life had ended when Jake disappeared, and it ended again when I believed he had died. But look at me now. Look at us now. I know you guys in the future probably think we're crazy for coming back here. That we've condemned ourselves to die thousands of years in the past just to save Jake. That it was foolish to give up the security and safety of the twenty-first century.

"But there are no guarantees in life. That's been true since the dawn of mankind. And if the four of us were meant to make it, we're going to make it anywhere. Anywhen."

Her eyes narrowed a bit as she leaned slightly closer to the camera. "And I hope you guys don't feel any guilt or responsibility over us being here because you showed me Jake's recordings. We all made this decision willingly and while I can't speak for Trish and Darren, I know I'm truly happy with it. Look at this amazing place! Whatever comes of this, we're facing it together. So for now I guess this is goodbye. I hope the next two cases have even more amazing content for you. Monsignor, Nic, Julien, Jean-Paul...I'll never forget you."

She blew a kiss at the camera and leaned forward, ending the recording.

At last it came to Jake's video. Father Julien paused to blow his nose before pressing play.

Jake leaned back onto the log after starting the recording, grimacing in pain from his injuries. "Well, I know I told everyone to record farewell messages, but I guess technically I already did mine on my phone a few days ago and now it's sealed in the brick over there. I gotta admit this is really surreal. You guys sharing my videos with Sara caused her and Darren and Trish to come back and save me. So in a way, you guys saved me. Thank you. It's a debt I can never repay, so I'll make sure we fill those other cases and provide you with whatever knowledge we can about this time, the animals, and any people we meet. This I swear to you."

As he spoke, a distant figure in the sky behind Jake gradually grew closer and closer until it was revealed to be an enormous whooping crane gliding low to the ground. It passed directly over Jake, casting a shadow. He looked up in surprise.

"Whoa! Did you see that! Holy shit this place is amazing! Wow." His eyes followed the bird off camera for several seconds before he turned back towards the camera and resumed speaking. "I...I don't really have anything else to say. So I guess we can just end it here."

Jake leaned forward and reached to the camera when he suddenly paused. "Wait a second," he said to himself before looking off camera. "Hey guys! We need to get a group shot with the camera before we pack it in!"

The video feed jostled as Jake pulled the camera out of the oak tree branches where it had apparently been wedged. He walked over to Sara and put the camera up on top of her head, revealing that everyone had been recording their farewell messages with Sara's helmet cam.

"Pass me the camera, please," Jake said.

Trish walked over and handed Jake a digital camera.

"Wait," Father Nic interrupted. "They had a regular camera with them this whole time?"

"I...I didn't know," Father Julien stuttered in surprise. "I was focussed on getting the video files decoded."

"Sara did mention taking photos a few times in the videos, but I didn't even think about it," Jean-Paul admitted.

Jake wedged the digital camera between the branches of the oak tree, taking care to orient it in the same angle that the helmet had been at for the confessionals. He called the others over and they walked up to the edge of the hill and lined up. Jake peered through the camera in the tree, now pointed at the group, set a timer, and ran over to the right of the scene. Sara turned her head to briefly look at Jake, then looked at Trish and Darren before facing the camera and holding her pose.

"One last time...say 'Cheese'!" Jake called.

"Cheese!" they all said in unison. A small LED on the camera in the tree blinked to indicate that the photo had been taken, and Jake walked back to the tree to retrieve the camera. He pulled it down and started looking at the preview screen on the back.

"How'd it turn out?" Darren asked.

"Perfect. We got it right on the first try. Good looking group!"

He walked up to Sara, his face filling the screen in the lab. "Now that's the right way to end this," he said, as reached up to the side of her head, ending the recording. The final frame of Jake's hand stretched to the screen receded back into the top-left corner of the grid.

Father Julien pressed the "next" button but a message popped up in the middle of the screen that read "no further media".

"That's it?" Jean-Paul said sadly, spinning in his chair and looking back at Father Julien.

Father Julien's voice cracked as he spoke. "That...that's all—" he said at first, then his face changed to a look of realization. "—for videos, that is!"

He exited the video playback software and opened up the file explorer, navigating through dozens of folders. "Aha! There were so many video files I didn't realize there was one folder of digital photos! One of the microSD cards was from that camera!"

He started bringing up the first photos in the folder. Test photos in Winnipeg, then photos of the island they initially swam to, along with close-ups of flowers, insects, and birds.

"Skip to the last file," Jean-Paul said impatiently.

Father Julien went to the bottom of the folder and opened the last image. It was the group photo they had just seen taken in the final video. That same beautiful vista, in high resolution, with visible giant bison in the background and flocks of birds in the partly cloudy, deep blue prairie sky. On the left was Jake, dressed in a clean T-Shirt and blue jeans that Sara must have brought for him, his bandaged arm around Sara's shoulder. Sara in turn looked young and alive, the bags that were under her eyes when she was in Rome having vanished. Beside her was Trish, who was wearing the dire wolf pelt as a headdress over her helmet and stood with her arm around Darren's waist. Darren stood tall and proud, his right arm around Sara and his left arm holding the barrel of his hunting rifle as the butt was on the ground. All four were smiling sincerely.

Father Julien left the photo up on the screen for a minute or so before he closed it and checked the remaining folders. "That's everything."

Jean-Paul looked at the Monsignor. "How can that be all? Did you open the other cases already...where are they?"

The Monsignor shook his head. "We do not have them."

Jean-Paul twisted his face in suspicion. "Wait, this isn't another one of those 'we have it but can't tell you because of protocol' things, is it?"

"I'm afraid not. Jacob Taylor's brick and the first case that they buried with it in the cairn are the only ones that made it to the reliquary," the Monsignor replied as he sank into his chair. "Until this moment we didn't even know there were other cases."

"So, the other cases didn't survive? Does that mean they died before they could bury them?" Jean-Paul asked dejectedly.

Father Nic spoke up as he wiped a tear from the corner of his eye. "Not necessarily. The boxes could have been found and are sitting in someone's private collection, in the archives of a local church, or in an attic somewhere. Not every religious relic gets sent to the Vatican."

Father Julien walked away from the podium and leaned against "It's also possible that those two boxes are still out there, undiscovered. Buried under ten thousand years of sediment or in a remote area not thoroughly explored or settled yet."

The Monsignor stared at the floor; his hands folded on his lap. "Even without highways or existing paths, it's possible to walk the breadth of North America within a year or two. Humans also stay by water so if they made it to a coast and buried the cases there, well...the coastline as it was ten thousand years ago would certainly be under water today."

"If they had found other people—" Father Nic mused. "Imagine if they got recordings of them...that would be one of the greatest archeological treasures ever! Recordings of languages that haven't been spoken for millennia, a glimpse at the first peoples of the Americas and their culture. It would be mind-blowing."

"What we've already seen has been mind blowing," Father Julien pointed out. All the men nodded in agreement.

"But what about the potential impacts to history?" Jean-Paul asked. "To the culture of whatever tribes they may have encountered? They had technology, medicine, and weapons from the twenty-first century. If they had kids or intermingled with the people of time...the genetics?"

The priests sat in silence considering his question. Finally, the Monsignor spoke. "Perhaps time is like an ocean. Four tiny pebbles were dropped into it ten thousand years ago and whatever ripples they caused have long since faded into the background noise of history."

"The Monsignor is right," Father Nic added. "Ten thousand years is a long time. Even if stories were told by their children, grandchildren, and great-grandchildren, it wouldn't be long before most of the details were distorted beyond recognition."

Father Julien folded his arms and looked towards the ceiling. "It's also possible that there was no impact. Maybe Trish was right. Maybe they were predestined to be there and have always been a part of our history. The reality is, we may never know."

After a few moments of silence, Jean-Paul spoke. "So, what now?"

"Now," the Monsignor groaned as he stood up out of his chair, placing a hand on his hip to support himself as he straightened up his back. "Now we resume our lives."

"But the other cases—" Jean-Paul stammered as he stood up along with him.

"They'll be searched for by other departments of the Vatican, I'm sure," the Monsignor answered. "Teams will be looking into historical records, private auction details, anything that might indicate that the cases were discovered in historical times.

He gestured to the other two priests. "As for us, our work here is done. We opened the brick and the case. We passed their messages on to the appropriate parties. It was just surprising that the appropriate parties turned out to be us."

"But—" Jean-Paul started to plead, then paused as he tried to think of some other angle to keep all of this going. "The wormhole! Or whatever it is that's linked to the past...what about it?"

"At present, the only people who are aware of its existence and exact location are His Holiness, a few key Cardinals, and the people in this room," Father Nic replied. "Our vows prohibit us from telling anyone, are we not planning on using it ourselves. I'd recommend you do the same. We feel that it's best to leave the past alone and look instead towards the future."

The Monsignor placed his hand on Jean-Paul's shoulder. "And don't forget, you signed the NDA. You know what will happen if you try to tell anyone about all this."

"But don't you need to know what happened to them? I know I do!"

"My son," the Monsignor spoke gently, lightly squeezing his shoulder. "The fact that we know as much as we do is a miracle. To the rest of the world, they're four unfortunate people who disappeared in the Canadian wilderness. That is how it must be."

"I think I could use a drink," Jean-Paul said, crestfallen.

Father Nic put his hands in his pockets and nodded. "I think we all could."

"It's settled then," the Monsignor announced boisterously, trying to change the mood of the room. "Let us return to the study."

"One moment," Father Julien interrupted. "*Signor* Ducharme, when Sara was here we gave her a copy of Jake's videos, since he intended them for her. As one of the recipients of these messages we can give you a copy of everything you've seen here today, just like we did for Sara. The NDA still applies, of course."

Jean-Paul paused for a moment and considered the offer. "I'm not sure, to be honest. Can I have more time to think about it?"

"Of course," the Monsignor said reassuringly. "Any time you want you can contact us."

Jean-Paul, Father Nic, and the Monsignor then left the lab together, returning up the musty staircase to the study, where the Monsignor opened his globe and pulled out a dusty and opened bottle of port.

He opened the bottle and poured a small amount into four glasses. "I only pull this out for special occasions. Today seems special enough to warrant it."

After Jean-Paul returned his temporary pass to Father Nic, the Monsignor handed them their glasses and they sat down facing each other.

The Monsignor raised his glass. "To Jacob Taylor."

"To Sara, Trish, and Darren," Jean-Paul added.

"May their days have been full of wonder and happiness," Father Nic concluded.

"God bless and keep them all," The Monsignor said as he made the sign of the cross. Father Nic quickly copied the gesture.

They touched their glasses together, took a sip, and then nursed their drinks in silence for a few minutes.

Father Nic pulled his cell phone out of his pocket. "I suppose I should arrange transport for *Signor* Ducharme." As he made a call and spoke quietly in Italian, Father Julien arrived from the secret passage, holding a piece of paper. He walked up to the group.

"While you make your decision about the rest of the data, I felt it was only right to run this through the printer for you."

He held out the piece of paper to Jean-Paul, who realized that it was a printout of the final photo the group had taken together, on high gloss photo paper. "Oh...wow...*Grazie*!" Jean-Paul sniffled.

Father Nic finished his call and put his cell phone back in his pocket. "A car will be here in ten minutes."

"It's funny," Father Julien said he picked up the glass the Monsignor had poured for him and took a drink. "Today is June...6th?" He pulled out his phone and looked at the clock. "*Madonna*! The time! I guess we're well into June 7th."

"And?" Father Nic asked.

Father Julien walked back over to the group and took another sip of port. "Well, the anomaly...whatever it is...it's in sync with the present, right? So almost everything we've just seen...technically it hasn't happened yet. Right now, Sara, Trish, and Darren have just started their journey. They won't find Jake until the 15th or 16th."

Father Nic put his hand to his forehead. "That hurts my head. I'm going to need another drink."

Father Julien chuckled. "What hurts my head are the gunshots. Sara heard Jake talk about 'fireworks' in his video three weeks ago, then went back in time and caused the noises he heard. So, was she fated to do this? Was that predestination?"

"Just stop," Father Nic pleaded.

Father Nic and Father Julien finished their drinks then went back to the globe for another round. They offered to refill Jean-Paul's near-empty tumbler, but he politely declined.

The Monsignor, who had been sitting in silence the whole time leaned towards Jean-Paul and spoke. "I know," he began slowly, carefully choosing his words, "that this entire situation has been...how do you say it in English? Messed up? I don't know how to feel about all this, and I've had a lifetime of preparation. I can't imagine how you feel right now."

Jean-Paul swallowed the last bit of port in his glass and put it down on the table, his eyes watching a droplet run down from the rim back to the bottom. "I don't know how I feel right now either. And you're right; it is messed up."

"If there is anything we can do for you," the Monsignor offered, placing his hand on Jean-Paul's arm.

Jean-Paul didn't take his eyes from the table. "That's just it; I wish there was something I could do. Three weeks ago, I didn't know any of these people existed. And now—"

The Monsignor smiled. "And now they are a part of us." Jean-Paul nodded.

A brief melodic tone from Father Nic's phone informed him that the car he ordered had arrived. Jean-Paul got up and embraced each priest before Father Nic walked him to the door where he shook hands with him.

"With no more ancient cases to open I suppose this is the last time we'll see each other?"

Father Nic shrugged his shoulders. "Who knows? Stranger things have certainly happened." He smiled half-heartedly.

"Good night, *Signor* Ducharme," he said as he slowly closed the door. "And God bless."

Jean-Paul bowed slightly then turned and walked to the street. He got into the back of the waiting car and sat there, lost in thought, until the impatient driver asked him in Italian what his destination was. He gave the address of his flat, then sat back into his seat and stared out the window for the entire journey. At no point did he even care enough to take his cell phone out of his pocket to check the time.

Epilogue

Jean-Paul only had a few hours of restless sleep in his bed before his alarm clock went off. He arose, showered, and got dressed. All this he did autonomously, as his mind was still going over the events of the night before. He was questioning whether everything he'd seen had been a dream, but sitting on his small table in his kitchen was the photograph Father Julien had printed out.

Hailing a taxi to take him to work, he sat in silence as the driver cursed at the morning traffic overtop the mix of American and European popular music playing over the radio. Arriving at the Consulate, Jean-Paul walked into the building and boarded the elevator. Arriving at his floor, he disembarked, acknowledging the greetings of a few of his coworkers with a slight nod.

As he walked past the break room he smelled the office coffee and realized he hadn't eaten a proper meal since he had been picked up by the lawyer and Gendarme the night before. He made himself a cup of coffee and grabbed a not-yet-stale bagel from a box of morning pastries. As he took a sip he walked to his desk, pondering just how many modern conveniences he was enjoying that Sara, Jake, Darren, and Trish never would again.

When he took the job at the Consulate, Jean-Paul had considered it an opportunity for adventure. But after a few months in Rome it had quickly become just another desk job in a city. Taking his seat he glanced over at his inbox, already stacked with a solid day's worth of paperwork. Grimacing he turned his gaze to his monitor and logged into his workstation.

Opening his email program his eyes scanned the new messages in his inbox. Tired and unable to focus, his eyes started to glaze over when they suddenly locked on to one new message from his cousin, Albert Ducharme, the RCMP officer from Manitoba who had put him in touch with Sara two weeks earlier. It had arrived late the previous night, Rome time, and the subject read "Sara Taylor". Jean-Paul furrowed his brow in curiosity and double-clicked on the message.

Dear Jean-Paul,

I hope you are doing well. We have recently started a missing persons investigation for Sara Taylor. Sara, along with Darren and Trish Reichert disappeared from their homes in Winnipeg two days ago. Darren's truck was found abandoned on highway 60 north of Cedar Lake, not far from where Jacob Taylor had disappeared last month. We are searching the area but no trace has been found of them so far.

We are still waiting on INTERPOL to get clearance to investigate the cellular signal from Jacob's phone in Rome. Did anything happen while Sara was there? Have you heard from her since she returned to Canada?

Albert

Jean-Paul stared at the message for several minutes before slowly moving the mouse cursor to overtop the "Reply" button. He was just about to click it when the phone on his desk rang. The caller ID display showed that it was his supervisor, Maria Adesina. He took his hand off his mouse, inhaled deeply, and answered the phone.

"Jean-Paul here."

"Good morning, Jean-Paul," Maria said in her melodic accent. "Can I see you in my office please?"

"Of course. I'll be right there," Jean-Paul replied before hanging up. He locked his workstation and left his desk, walking down a hall containing a row of low-walled cubicles, each with a busy consulate employee at work. When he reached Maria's office, the door was closed so he knocked.

"Enter," Maria called from behind the door.

As Jean-Paul walked in, he first saw Maria sitting at her desk. She was smartly dressed in a woman's business suit, and her long hair was tucked up into a traditional Nigerian hat. His eyes were quickly drawn from her to the bright red robes worn by a cardinal of the Catholic church sitting in her guest chair on the right. Upon his entrance, both Maria and the cardinal stood up, and the cardinal extended his ringed hand.

"Jean-Paul, this is Cardinal Augusta," Maria said, then turned to the cardinal. "Jean-Paul Ducharme, Your Eminence."

Overcoming the surprise of the situation, Jean-Paul remembered his etiquette, took the cardinal's outstretched hand, bowed and kissed his ring. "Your Eminence," he said politely.

Maria and Cardinal Augusta sat back in their chairs, and Jean-Paul joined them next to the cardinal. "I've been having the most interesting conversation with the cardinal this morning," Maria began as she looked slyly at Jean-Paul. "I had no idea you were so involved with the Church."

A look of puzzlement crossed Jean-Paul's face as he glanced between Maria and the cardinal. "I'm sorry, I have no idea what you mean."

"*Signora* Adesina, if I may have a moment with *Signor* Ducharme?" Cardinal Augusta requested, smiling gently.

"Of course, Your Eminence," Maria said. Standing up, she took her cell phone off her desk and left the office, closing the door behind her. The moment the door was closed the cardinal's smile vanished.

"*Signor* Ducharme," he said sternly. "Do you know why I'm here?"

"No, Your Eminence."

"I am here...because the Church would like to offer you a job," he said, pointing at Jean-Paul.

"A job? I don't understand. What kind of job?"

The cardinal put his elbows on the armrests of his chair and folded his fingers together. "The kind that involves tracking down religious artifacts and returning them to the Church."

Jean-Paul's eyes went wide. "The other two cases," he said in a hushed tone.

"*Si, Signor* Ducharme."

"Why me?"

"The Holy See has decided that it is of extreme importance to find and retrieve those artifacts. However, the existence of these artifacts is still a secret known only by a handful of men here in Rome. Given there is a good chance that they may be in North America it would be helpful to have a North American involved. As you are a Canadian who already has knowledge of these artifacts, you're a logical choice for the team. You will operate out of Vatican City effective immediately."

Jean-Paul was shocked. "But...I'm a Canadian citizen and I'm employed here at the Consulate."

"All the paperwork has already been taken care of," the cardinal said nonchalantly. "The Catholic Church invented bureaucracy; we know how to cut through it."

Overwhelmed, Jean-Paul brought his left hand up to this temple and massaged it. "This is all happening so fast—"

"*Signor* Ducharme," the cardinal said in a tone of utmost seriousness. "Last night you told Monsignor Wowchuk that you wanted to help...that you needed to know what happened to the Taylors and the Reicherts, did you not?"

Jean-Paul swallowed hard. "I did."

Cardinal Agusta leaned towards Jean-Paul. He raised his eyebrows and opened his hands. "Well then, now's your chance."

Jean-Paul gripped the arms of his chair and stared off in the distance, considering his options. After what felt like an eternity, he slowly met the cardinal's gaze.

"What do I need to do?"

"Clean out your desk. There's a car waiting for you downstairs. Send *Signora* Adesina back in and I will take care of the rest."

"*Grazie*, Your Eminence!" Jean-Paul said, reaching for the cardinal's ringed hand.

Cardinal Augusta waved him away dismissively. "Yeah, yeah. Just go. *Tempus fugit!*"

Jean-Paul left Maria's office and walked back towards his desk. He passed her talking to one of his coworkers and told her that the cardinal wished to speak to her further. He finally reached his workspace and plopped down into his chair. He had very few personal effects and grabbed a plastic bag he kept in a drawer to pack them up in. He spun in his chair to leave but at the last minute glanced back at the computer. Rolling back up to his keyboard he unlocked his workstation where the email from his cousin was still on the screen.

He hit the "Reply" button then paused for a moment while the cursor blinked awaiting his reply.

```
Dear Albert,


Sorry,  I  haven't  heard  from  Sara
since  she  left  Rome.  I'll  let  you
know  if  anything  changes.


Jean-Paul


PS - I may be a little hard to reach
for the next while.
```

Jean-Paul hit the send button, locked the computer, picked up his box, and walked out of the Consulate. Waiting for him across the street was the same black Renault that had picked him up the evening before. As he got into the back, he was only mildly surprised to see Frau Something-or-Other in the seat beside him looking at her cell phone.

"Hello again," Jean-Paul said to her. She curled her upper lip slightly in response but otherwise didn't acknowledge him. He didn't bother attempting to make any smalltalk for the drive back to Vatican City.

After a now-familiar drive he found himself once again being let out in front of the same flat as the previous two times. Father Nic was already waiting at the open door and led him and the lawyer to the study.

As the stack of legal papers were dropped in front of him, Jean-Paul rolled his eyes. "A third time? This is getting old."

"This time it's different," Father Nic said with a smile, and he pulled out an ID card on a lanyard with Jean-Paul's name on it. Unlike the previous two cards he had received, this one did not say "*provisio*".

Jean-Paul inhaled deeply. "Let's do this."

He began signing and initialling documents. Once all the pages were filled out and witnessed, Frau Something-or-Other exited the study and Father Nic led Jean-Paul down to the laboratory. The normally clean space was now cluttered, filled with books, computers, tablets, and display cases with artifacts in them. Father Nic patted him on the back and went to one of the stations where he started paging through large volumes and checking information on his tablet, resuming work he had previously stopped to see Jean-Paul in.

The Monsignor and Father Julien then entered from one of the side rooms. Upon seeing Jean-Paul, the Monsignor's face lit up and he walked up and embraced Jean-Paul. "Welcome, welcome!"

"Thank you. What is all this?"

"It turns out the Holy See's desire for secrecy surrounding the cases is pretty absolute," the Monsignor replied. "So there is only one main team that knows everything: this one. And it consists of me, Fathers Nicolas and Julien, and of course, you."

"But why the rush? Why is this all happening now?"

"If you recall, the two remaining cases were marked with instructions to be opened tomorrow and in two days. If someone else has them in their possession they may choose to open them, if they haven't already."

Father Julien brought up a map onto the projector screen and pointed at it. There were markers of different colours on the map. "We've already started compiling maps of what North America looked like ten thousand years ago based on data from the United

States Geological Survey, Natural Resources Canada, and every major university in North America. That should help us narrow down possible locations that the four travelled to in their lifetimes."

"You know how to do that?" Jean-Paul asked, impressed.

Father Julien laughed. "Me? No. But we have the full power of the Holy See behind us so basically whatever we ask for, we get, no questions asked. I told some people I wanted this map, and they started making it."

"What do the different colours mean?" Jean-Paul asked him, pointing at the markers on the map.

"Green is for locations we definitely know they were at, such as their point of ingress at the Walter Cook Upland Cave Reserves, and Stony Mountain. Yellow is where we believe certain events took place."

"And the blue markers?"

"Blue marks places of interest, where evidence of ancient human occupation has been found. As you can see there are several in the badlands of South Dakota which would have certainly been reachable by the Taylors and Reicherts within a few months of their arrival."

"Wow," Jean-Paul said, a little overwhelmed with everything going on. He walked back over to the Monsignor who was clicking through Sara's photos on a laptop. "I guess you're in charge here, yes?"

"No," the Monsignor replied, as he poked Jean-Paul in the chest with his index finger. "You are."

"What?! Why me?"

"My place is here with the artifacts, and Father Julien will be staying with me and coordinating the I.T. side of things. As our resident North American, and a 'consultant' to The Vatican, you'll get us access to places where we don't necessarily want the Church's presence known."

Jean-Paul gripped the back of a nearby chair. "Christ! What have I signed up for?"

"Don't worry, you won't be alone. Father Nicolas will accompany you wherever you need to go, whether it's Sao Paulo, or South Dakota."

"Did someone say 'South Dakota'?" Father Nic suddenly said, lifting his head from this tablet. He started digging through the piles of books and publications on his table before finding what he was looking for. He then went through the various open tabs on his tablet to find some matching information.

"The badlands in South Dakota have been inhabited for at least eleven thousand years. Did you know that there's an ancient skull in the University of South Dakota's anthropology department that appears to have a bullet hole above the left eye?"

"A bullet hole?!" He looked at the map and all the blue markers in South Dakota.

The Monsignor put his hand on Jean-Paul's shoulder. "What do you say, *Signor* Ducharme? What is our first move?"

"Yeah, you're the boss, *Signor* Ducharme," Father Julien echoed.

Jean-Paul looked down for a moment pensively, then looked back up at the three men in the room.

"Let's go check out that skull," he said as the three priests smiled at him. "And please, my friends call me JP."

About the Author

Clayton Rumley makes his debut into the Canadian literature scene with his first book of the Holocene trilogy. An introverted software developer by day, he is also a composer, photographer, indie video game developer, YouTuber, and the creator behind the popular website Drawn. He lives in his hometown of Winnipeg, Manitoba, Canada with his wife and children and almost never sleeps.